This book is dedicated to the City of Sydney

Also by Rob Alexander

The Landing Craft
Darwin's Eden
The Hack
The GenStar Saga

THE HACK

Rob Alexander

JumpFish Publishing

Sydney

First published January 2025 by JumpFish Publishing.

This edition, January, 2025.

ISBN-13: 978-0-9945792-4-9

9 8 7 6 5 4 3

A CIP catalogue record for this book is available from the Australian Library.

Printed and bound by Ingram Spark.

Acknowledgements

I extend my gratitude to Claire Dielenberg for her occasional observations, which helped identify minor inconsistencies in the manuscript and contributed to its refinement. I'd also like to thank Todd Archer for inventing the name 'Reg Faraday.' It proved useful in a couple of chapters. I'd also like to thank Pascal Carrive again for his contribution to proofreading and cover art, and Itoe Mori for her suggestions to improve the cover art.

"Cuando no tengo azul, pongo rojo."

– Pablo Picasso, *Libération* (1976) –

– 1 –

The Light Brigade Hotel
Woollahra, Sydney, 1993

"SHE was a rising starlet with a whale-sized ambition, but all of that was snuffed out one night when she decided to prostitute herself to tie the rent over."

Finn didn't say anything, he just stared at Zac with an expression that said, *Ok, I'm going to shake my head now*. But he didn't.

It was in his eyes. And Zac knew he had him.

"Go on."

"She picked up this guy in a bar. You know, the kind of guy whose flab hangs over his belt, a typical office guy who —"

"— Where does she pick him up?"

Zac smiled. "Sweethearts of course."

"Of course."

"So anyway, they get talking. You know, he buys her a drink.

She accepts. He asks what she does. She's an actress looking for work. It's tough with the recession and everything."

"So this is set in the present?"

"Uh-huh."

Finn took a sip of his beer. Victoria Bitter. Writer's beer Zac called it. Finn wasn't one to disagree. He leaned on most things Zac said. "So what happened then?"

"This is where it gets interesting ... he takes her down to his yacht on the harbour. He lets her inspect it. The fine wood-work. The brass fittings. The spacious galley. He shows her the 'captain's quarters' up in the bow. It's cozy and well appointed. There's shelves for books on each side, and some storage cabinets. The sheets are Chinese silk. A skylight lets starlight in."

Finn rotated his glass.

"She sat on the bed, nervously picking the cuticle of her thumb with her index finger. He watched her, his expression noncha-lant. He's done this countless times. 'Five hundred,' she says. Her eyes darken at this point. Her pupils have dilated. He's seen this all before. He pretends to be shocked at the price. He's never coughed up more than a hundred bucks for a fuck. Some of them were even skanks with track marks. This one is fresh. Like a newborn deer in the headlights. 'What's so special about you that makes a price like that worth it?' 'I need the money ...' she looks around, 'and you can afford it. You're not going to go cheap on me are you?' she says, pretending to be coy."

Finn chuckled. He liked her sass.

"'In that case,' he says, 'I'll make it worth it.' He reaches across her body and opens a small cabinet and pulls out some rope. She can feel his heat and smell the rancid odor of sweat through his shirt. 'It's sheet rope, for winding winches,' he says, taking her wrists firmly—his fingernails bitten down to the quick—she shudders but submits."

Zac took another sip of his beer while he considered the next lines. "He tied the rope firmly around her wrists, not so tight as to cut her blood circulation off, but tight enough to let her know this was serious. She straightened her fingers out, palms together, but he looped the rope between them, knotted it off. There was no way she could slip her hands out now. Did I tell you his name?—"

"No."

"It's Wilford. Thomas Wilford."

"What does he do?"

"He's a successful architect. He has some underlings and so he mostly just consults now."

"And he's into bondage."

Zac betrayed the slightest suggestion of a smile. "He's into a lot more than that mate."

Finn waited for the penny to drop.

"Without any fanfare, he pushes her back down on the bed, reaches up her mini-skirt and yanks her panties down—so they're wrapped around her knees, which he raises up, so he can see her pussy. He likes that, the knees together and the feet splayed out. He stares at her for a while, taking it in, not leering or anything like that. It's more of a professional look, like a wine connoisseur trying to decide on which bottle he'll take. Her pussy is neat, not too hairy, the lips glistening pink."

"What did you say her name was?"

"I didn't." Zac took a moment to think about it. Nodding to himself, he says, "Whinnie."

"Whinnie?"

"Yeah, why not?"

"It's kind of old-fashioned."

"She's a starlet. All starlets are old-fashioned. It's how they started out."

"Like the 1920s."

"Yeah, like the 1920s."

"Go on."

"He sticks his finger into her pussy to see if it's wet. It is. She makes a little sound in her throat. It's not pleasure. Nor is it surprise. It's the kind she'd make when the dentist hits a raw nerve. Satisfied, he pulls her back upright, directs her hands to his fly. She obliges him and liberates his member."

"His member?"

"What do you want me to say? His cock? I'm trying to narrate a story here."

"How about his 'Johnson?'"

"He's not in the military. He's a business man. Well-educated."

"Fair enough."

Zac took another draught of his beer. "Where was I?"

"She's sucking his cock."

"Right. It's not like she hasn't sucked cock before, but he doesn't like the way she goes about it. She's too tentative. He likes it rough. He grabs the back of her head and thrusts her face into his pubic hair, and holds her there while he thrusts hard into her. He holds her like that until she jerks back violently, heaving for air. He sees the surprise and fear in her eyes and it turns him on. Whinnie realizes for the first time what she's got herself into. What—?"

"—Where do you get this stuff?"

Zac gives him a straight look. "Do you wanna to hear the rest of the story, or are you going to keep interrupting me?"

"Nah, go on."

Zac says, "He forces her to deep throat him again, and again—and she's thinking the whole time it'll be over soon and she can go home and have a hot shower. But he withdraws and goes into the galley and gets a knife. It's Japanese. Sharper than a razor blade. 'You know what I use this for?' he says. 'Filleting fish.' And this time his expression is leery. Her eyes widen with fear. 'I need to pee,' she says. He leans forward, strokes the blade against her cheek. 'The toilet's down there. Don't try anything funny.' He's letting her go to the toilet you see, because he doesn't want her urinating all over his fine woodwork. He has a sense of decorum."

"How nice of him."

"Inside the toilet, Whinnie tries to undo the rope around her wrists, but he's done a good job. She's thinking: *he's just messing around. He likes scaring girls, but he doesn't hurt them.* At least that's one part of her brain. The other part is telling her to get out of there. Get out of there now!"

Finn is nodding.

"He calls after her. 'What's taking you so long?' 'I'll just be a minute,' she says. He fingers the edge of the blade. He thinks it could do with a bit of sharpening. Just then, she bursts out of the door and makes a run for it. The stairs leading up and out of the galley into the cockpit are right there. She climbs them real fast before his mind registers what's going on. He has a flash image of stabbing her in the back, but he doesn't act on it. It's not what he planned. Instead, he puts the knife down on the galley table and rushes as her and grabs her legs. There is a momentary struggle. He shouts at her to 'calm down.' But she's anything but calm. She screams for help and tries to kick him off. But he's got a good hold of her and he yanks her back with a great force. She falls onto him, into his arms, and he staggers backwards ... together they crash into the galley stove. It pivots violently. Unbeknownst to him, the gas line snaps. She bites his arm and he roars with pain. He rages and throws her across the galley table. She tumbles over it, but is back on her feet as quick as an alley cat. He steps in front of her and blocks her way. She freezes and desperately looks around, and lucky for her, she finds the knife on the floor. It surprises her. A gift from the heavens. She snatches it up and holds it between her hands—which are still bound—

brandishing it at him. 'Get out of my way!' she cries. 'What do you think you're gonna do with that?' he asks. He's speaking to her in a fatherly tone now. Like he's talking to a little child. 'Let me go,' she says. 'Give it to me,' he says. She makes a stabbing motion, thinking it will deter him. He looks around and he sees his raincoat hanging on a hook behind the stairs. There's a closet there. He grabs it and says, 'I'm going to take the knife off you now.' She's thinking, I did this in acting school. It was a wooden knife then, but the principle is the same. He's gonna to come at me, try to smother me. Stab, stab, stab! Attack first. She launches herself at him. He flourishes the coat in an attempt to stop her. It swirls through the air like a matador's cape. And then his mouth falls open in a silent gasp. The knife is sticking out of his belly. They look at each other, dumbstruck. She lets go and sinks to the ground. He doesn't know what to do. He's never been in this situation before. It hurts. Something inside is wrong. He doesn't know why, but he pulls the knife out in one clean motion. He moans in pain. He sees the blood gush out and he nearly faints. He drops the raincoat and puts his hand over the wound. He stays like that for a moment, seeing if he can steady himself. The whole time Whinnie hasn't moved. She's frozen. She's never stabbed a person before. She didn't feel the blade go in. It was more like a punch. It all happened so fast. 'I'm gonna kill you!' he growls. 'I'm gonna kill you!' He moves toward her, takes a step. But he's not going anywhere. 'Cause he slips on his raincoat! He throws out his hand to grab onto something. It's the edge of the galley table. The knife flies out of his hand and hits a brass fitting, and then—kaboom! There's a blinding flash of light and a massive pressure wave. It happens in the blink of an eye. The windows are blown out. The cabin doors fly off their hinges. The curtains catch fire. Whinnie is thrown back into the captain's quarters. Wilford hits the ceiling then falls back to the floor like a pancake."

"Jesus."

"The fire rapidly takes hold. The nautical charts which were rolled up and stored in tubes alongside the galley table begin burning. As do the books in the small shelves over the galley bunk. The curtains are the worst; they go up like tissue paper. Smoke fills the cabin. Wilford isn't moving. Whinnie crawls up to him, shakes him but he doesn't respond. She makes a half-hearted attempt to drag him towards the stairs, thinking maybe she can save him—but it's futile. He's like a beached whale. The knife is laying nearby. She grabs it and makes her way up the stairs, the smoke billowing around her as she goes. Up on the deck she uses the knife to cut through the rope. She does it by kneeling with the knife between her knees, rubbing her hands back and forth until she frees herself. The flames at this stage are licking around her like snakes' tongues. She makes her way to the stern, where the small dingy that Wilford used to ferry them to the yacht is tied off. She pulls it in, climbs over the railing and lowers herself down, but her hands slip and she hits the rubber side and falls into the water. She's too weak to pull herself into the dingy and after a few tries, gives up. She hangs there onto the dingy as it drifts to the end of its tether. She doesn't know how long she can hold on, she's growing weaker by the moment. As luck would have it, someone comes in another dingy and picks her up."

"So it's a complete disaster," Finn murmured.

"Pretty much. The ambulance comes soon after. They take her to The Royal North Shore. Emergency doctors assess her and immediately put her into an induced coma. She has third degree burns to nearly seventy percent of her body. She has no ID on her, so they end up calling her the 'boat lady.' The incident is reported in the news, but no one comes forth to claim her. The police are miffed. They quickly identify the boat as belonging to one Thomas Wilford, of 43 Comber Street Paddington, and question his wife, Margaret. They have a son, nineteen, going to uni, but other than that, nothing remarkable. They look into Wilford's business. He has an office in Surry Hills, three employees. They do small office buildings and townhouses. Behind the scenes, of course, things are different ..."

"His wife would want to know what Wilford was doing with the girl."

"Absolutely."

"So what's your take on that?"

"Well, if you think about it, it all depends on her personality. She's a stay-at-home wife, not too smart, but not too dumb either. She spends part of her life working as a secretary for Wilford, but she got diagnosed with breast cancer and had to undergo treatment. Luckily they caught it early thanks to the introduction of breast screening in New South Wales around that time. But they had to remove one of her breasts."

"Right."

"Their son, Mathew, he wants to forget about the whole thing. Wilford's business has to be sold, and he's going to get a nice inheritance. Margaret gets a sizable payout from his insurance policy. The case is never solved, and it's soon forgotten by all."

"Except ..."

"Except Detective Frank Badger."

"Ah-ha, so this is where it starts."

"I forgot to mention, Whinnie ..."

"Yeah?"

"She didn't make it."

"Oh."

"No. She has to die."

"Why?"

"Because it adds to the mystery."

"Right. So what's the mystery?"

"That's the part I'm coming to."

Finn took a long swig of his beer. Listening to all this was making him thirsty.

"Wilford, you see—well, you probably guessed—this is not the first time he's done this."

"For sure."

"In fact ... he's done it to seven other girls."

"Yeah, right! I see where this is going."

"No you don't."

Finn wanted to argue, but Zac wouldn't have any of it. He said, "Badger—as per his name—he's not going to let this one go. Seven other girls found floating in Sydney Harbour—at least what was left of them after the bull sharks got to them. So he's definitely not a happy camper. Because he hasn't found out who's doing this. But now ... with this break, he's thinking ... right, he's got something. Except all the evidence is destroyed, and the only potential witness, well, she's dead."

"So he picks on Margaret, because he thinks she knows something."

"You're learning my friend."

"But Margaret doesn't know anything."

"She's clueless."

"Right."

"Badger can't get a search warrant, because he hasn't got probable cause. He'd love nothing more than to turn Wilford's house upside down. He's sure that Wilford kept souvenirs."

"So Wilford is a classic serial killer."

"Sort of. But we'll get to that."

"Ok."

"The thing is, Badger is not getting any love from his Sergeant. His mind is made up. He thinks the killer is the postman."

"The postman?" Finn laughs raucously. "You're joking, right?"

"I know, it's a total cliche. But you've got to have at least one twist in your story."

"Ah, so there's a twist. I was waiting for that."

"There's an art to the twist ..."

"I'm hopeless at them."

"So am I. Not all of us are born Agatha Christie."

"I haven't read any of her stuff ..."

"Neither have I."

They both laugh and drain the last of their beers. Finn offers to shout the next round. He brings back another two schooners of VB.

"So where were we?" Zac asks again, taking the froth off the top of his beer, sucking it with his lips. They're full lips, plump with youthful vigor.

"Badger is getting shafted."

Zac nods. "Yeah, big time. You see, the postman, his run is Balmoral, and according to Badger's Sergeant, there was a witness saying she saw the posty—let's call him John Bannister—lurking around Obelisk Beach—the opposite side of Balmoral—pretty much where the currents would take a body out to sea."

"Where did Wilford moor his boat?"

"Balmoral."

"Right."

"Coincidence, yeah?"

"Yeah."

"But it gets worse. John was also last seen with one of the prostitutes."

"So they're all prostitutes?"

"It's Wilford's M.O. He thinks no one will ever notice them missing."

"But they do."

"Yeah, some of them. Because they're someone's daughter. Someone's mother. Someone's wife."

"For sure."

"The thing is, ever since Margaret had that breast operation, she changed. She's not interested in sex any more. She's completely turned off by it."

"Is this your ploy to get sympathy for Wilford?"

"Not really. I'm just telling it as it is."

"Fair enough."

"So they pick this John guy up, and they interrogate him."

"This is Badger's Sergeant?"

"Yeah."

"And even though they don't have DNA testing yet, they take blood and hair samples, and low-and-behold, they find one of John's hair's stuck in a woollen jumper that one of the prostitutes was wearing. They found a torso still clad in a jumper. A pink jumper."

"Wilford wasn't a breast man."

"No," Zac says, giving him a dead-pan look.

'Talk about bad luck. What did he do? Did he go with this prostitute?"

"That's what it looks like."

"Jesus."

"So they're sure they've got their man. They take him to trial. He gets convicted. They put him away for life."

"Fuck me."

"But don't forget, Wilford is dead. So now the murders stop."

"Right. Talk about timing."

"Exactly."

"That's nasty."

"Wait for it, it gets a lost nastier."

Finn took a quick sip of his beer. He was getting into this.

"Several years go by. Mathew finishes university. He decides he wants to go to Europe before starting work. He's been using his dad's car, and he asks his mum if he can park it in the garage while he's away. She ums-and-ahs, the garage is full of shit. She has to clean it out if the car is going to fit. Mathew helps her and they move a bunch of boxes and things, bring them inside the house. Mathew parks his car and heads off to Europe."

"Ok."

"They put them in the sun room, which is kind of a junk room anyway. A few days later she's watering one of the pot plants there and she accidentally spills some water over one of the boxes. It seeps inside. Worried, she opens it up and sees a bunch of stuff in there, some old crockery and glasses. There's a shoe box in there; the water has collected on top of it. She gets a dish cloth and wipes it dry. Curious, she gets it out and opens it up to see what's inside. She expecting cutlery or something like that, but instead, it's full of women's underwear. For a moment she just stares at them; her brain freezes. Perhaps she's thinking they're hers from way back when. She starts taking them out and looks at them. She doesn't recognize any of them. Then she see a notebook in there that was hidden underneath them. Her heart starts pounding hard in her chest. She takes it out and opens it, and immediately recognizes her husband's handwriting ... the words swim in front of her eyes:

"It's impossible to say how it started ... maybe it's a genetic thing, or something I experienced in the womb, but slowly, like the layers of an onion being peeled away, this dark, brutal impulse was exposed. It was like staring into a black hole, it drew me in. I couldn't resist it. I mean, I tried. God I tried. But it kept pulling me in. At first, I pretended it wasn't happening. But then I found myself cruising the Cross. Looking. Hunting. And so I gradually succumbed to it. I began to start planning. The same way I planned an architectural drawing. From the ground up. Left nothing to chance. The first time, I took one down and just fooled around. I let her go. The second one I experimented with a bit of rope play. I let her go as well. But the third one, I went all the way. Her name was Lisa. And it was nothing like I imagined. In fact, it was a bit of a downer. I swore then and there that the next one would be perfect. No more mistakes. I was hooked. I could no longer deny it. And so I've taken to calling it My Secret Disease ..."

Finn repeated the words: "My Secret Disease."

"That's what I'm calling this."

"So he left a journal of his exploits."

"Pretty much."

"So what does she do? Take it to the police?"

"Absolutely not! And for good reason."

"It's too hard for her to digest I guess."

"It's not just that. She's thinking of Mathew. He can never know anything about it. She doesn't want to ruin his life."

"Yeah, right."

"But she's got this problem now. She knows that this other guy—John—is innocent. It starts eating at her. But she can't bring herself to do anything. She's already thrown the panties in the trash. And she's planning to burn the journal before Mathew gets back. But ..."

"She's reading it ..."

"Oh yeah. She reads it like the Bible. Sickened by every word but she can't put it down."

"Real life is stranger than fiction."

"You bet it is."

"So he recorded every victim, every detail?"

"Pretty much."

"Man, that's gonna take a twisted mind ..."

Zac shrugged and took a gulp of his beer. "Humans have been killing each other every which way since time immemorial. What's Wilford gonna do that's original? It's all been done before."

"You're thinking of—what's his name?"

"Who?"

"I donno. Marquis de Sade."

Zac smiled. "Now that guy was a deviant. Wilford by comparison is just your regular garden variety psychopath. But you see—it doesn't matter what he does. So long as he does it in secret, and so long as it involves sex and murder. People can't get enough of that shit. That's why it has to be this way."

"You're a fucken deviant."

"I don't get into that shit. I just dream it up."

"So what happened to the wife? What does she do with the journal?"

"I tell you what she does. She writes an anonymous letter to John Bannister. She includes information from Wilford's journal on some of the victims, only things that he could have known. Specific details, like a birth mark that one of the victims had just above her right kidney. The prison of course has to censor each letter before they hand it over to inmates. When they read this letter they go ballistic. Their first reaction is to cover it up. But John's lawyer gets wind of it. Because John has been mounting an appeal. It hits the news big time. Margaret should be relieved, right?"

"Yeah, she did the right thing."

"She did, but her doctor tells her that her cancer's back. And this time it's gone to her liver, her bones, her brain."

"Oh."

"Yeah, it's not good, and so she decides to burn the journal in case she can't afterwards. She gathers up the ashes, and takes them to Wilford's grave-site in Rookwood Cemetery. He has a small plot there with a headstone. Margaret says, 'We promised to be buried side-by-side. Well I'm breaking that promise. No! You broke it.' And she tips the ashes over his grave and spits on them. On the way back she collapses in her driveway. She is taken to St. Vincent's. Mathew cuts his Europe trip short—he was planning to spend a year there—and rushes to her bedside. She is in a private room, with a TV. The news comes out that John Bannister's conviction has been quashed. The police make a plea for the person who wrote the anonymous letter. Mathew notices his mother, who a short while earlier was almost half comatose, is now lucid, her attention riveted to the screen. He says, 'What is it? Are you all right?' She says, 'I'm proud of you Mathew. You're nothing like your father. You have your own life, and I know you're going to do great.' Mathew senses she is telling him something, but he can't figure it out. He sees the body bags being taken from the harbour, the grim-faced police taciturn, then looks back at his mother. She is pointing to something in her bedside drawer. Mathew opens the drawer and finds an envelope. She tells him to open it. There is a note inside. He reads it:

I wish that my remains be cremated. I trust my son Mathew will ensure that my wish is granted.

He looks up, and sees that Margaret's eyes have closed, and she is very still. He shakes her, 'Mum, mum!' A nurse comes in and takes Margaret's pulse. The nurse tells Mathew that she has passed."

"Bloody hell."

———— • ————

"Literary fiction, my arse!" Those were the words that came out of Zac's mouth before the start of all of this.

Finn had heard it all before. Zac didn't just despise literary fiction. He felt it was his duty to shit on it, whenever and wherever he could.

And today was no different. Outside, the sky was a brilliant cerulean blue, dotted with just a few cotton wool clouds, barely a wisp of wind, while the boys hunkered down inside the Light Brigade Hotel, a world away from it all. They weren't interested in the adventures that lay beyond the horizon. They were too busy cooking up their own in the cauldron of their imaginations.

And as usual, the conversation quickly turned into a pissing contest. Who could marshal the strongest evidence in favor of their respective positions.

Finn firmly believed that commercial fiction wasn't merely a superficial escape for bored housewives and holiday makers, but an essential art form that illuminated people's dreams—even the mundane or absurd ones. After all, what did people have but their dreams? He completely rejected the notion that human progress diminishes the mystery of life. To him, the mystery was boundless, and writers could explore its depths wherever and whenever they wished. If that resulted in crap, then that was the writer's fault, not the art form.

Zac didn't disagree in principle, but he despised the insular provincialism that dominated the literary market. The way it pandered to minority groups as if there was such a thing as a majority group when it came to merit.

As usual, Finn made him spell it out.

"You want me to say it?" Zac challenged.

"Yeah."

"Ok, I'll tell you what literary fiction is," he said. "It's a toad dressed in pyjamas."

Finn just stared at him.

Zac laughed. "You thought I was going to get on my hobby horse."

Finn gave Zac a dissatisfied look.

Zac merely shrugged.

Finn gruffed and said, "So what's a toad doing dressed in pyjamas?"

"It's a metaphor dude."

"Yeah, I know that. But what are you trying to say?"

"You've heard the phrase 'the emperor has no clothes,' right?"

"Yeah I've heard it. But I'm not sure what it means. I mean, I think I know what it means, but you'll tell me I've got it wrong for sure."

"At least have a guess."

Finn rubbed the corners of his mouth. "A guess ... I suppose it means the rich and powerful are all surface appearance, when you take their clothes off they're just like us."

Zac gave Finn a moment to dwell on what he had just said, then said, "It's sort of right, but it misses the point."

"What's the point then?"

"The original idea, if you want to know, came from Hans Christian Anderson. We're talking about the 1800s. Fairytales, that sort of thing. Anderson wrote a story in which a king was hoodwinked by weavers into believing his suit of clothes could only be seen by people who are intelligent."

"It appeals to his ego."

"Yeah, the king was fooled into believing he was above the commoners."

"Yeah."

"Same as literary fiction."

Finn rubbed his chin. "Hmm, not quite. It's more subtle than that. In fairy tales, the toad often gets transformed into a prince, so it's saying that literary fiction can transform it into royalty if given a 'kiss' by the right person—"

"—But they're still wearing pyjamas!"

They both laughed heartily.

"But hey," Zac said, "pyjamas can also be a symbol of the rich and wealthy."

"Oh yeah," Finn said, "prancing around in pyjamas while drinking cocktails, I've seen that."

"You would," Zac said, more seriously.

Finn gauged Zac's comment and said, "Come on mate. You know as well I do it's all bullshit."

"Oh yeah, I know it's bullshit," Zac said. "That's why I don't buy into it."

"So why did you do English Literature in the first place?" Finn said. He meant it seriously.

"I dunno," Zac said, looking into his glass. "I'm not sure any more."

"Come on mate! That's not you."

"Is it?"

"Yeah! I've been telling all my friends you're a genius. That you'll write a classic one day."

Zac couldn't help laughing at himself. "Mate, I stopped believing I was a genius long ago."

Finn grinned foolishly. "While I ... am just warming up to the idea."

"I'll drink to that!" Zac said raising a salute.

They drained their glasses.

Finn went and fetched another round. Setting the glasses down, he said, "I can see by that look in your eyes that you're thinking of a new story. Are you gonna share it with me?"

Zac deflected, tried to shake Finn off.

"Come on," Finn pressed. "Or is the world not good enough for you?"

They locked gazes. It wasn't antagonistic. It was the competitiveness again.

Zac rubbed his chin. It was peppered with a coarse stubble. The color of roasted coffee beans. It made him look intense— when he wasn't smiling. It was the kind of intensity that Finn associated with real writers. Writers that were born writers, not the wanna-be's who appropriated the image for self-gratification.

Finn was practically his polar opposite. Sandy blonde hair, the kind that frizzes up after shampooing. So he kept it short to manage it. His eyes were gray-blue, like his father's. His face, however, was more like his mother's. A model's face. Fine-boned and somewhat delicate. He could have gone into acting and it wouldn't have hurt him.

Zac took a deep draught of his beer, wiped his lips, and said, "Ok, so you want something?"

Finn said, "Yeah. Let's hear it."

– 2 –

Fairfax Building

Ultimo, Sydney

"R EG wants to see you."

It was Martha Kensington, gossip columnist, who was walking past Dick Garret's desk as she dropped the news.

"What—now?"

"Now!"

"Jeez," Garret swore under his breath. He was busy doing a crossword puzzle and didn't want to be disturbed. He was waiting for a phone call. It could be the break he was looking for. He put his 2B pencil down, pulled himself out of his chair, and stalked his way over to Reg Faraday's office.

'Reginald Faraday, Editor-in-Chief' was stenciled on the glass paneled door. Garret knocked gently, and let himself in.

Faraday was just getting off the phone. He motioned Garret

to sit down. The room was small for an editor-in-chief, the desk stacked high with copy. Windows let him see out as far as Sydney University's quadrangle, and across the bullpen where he could keep an eye on 'his' journos as they sweated out their daily grind.

Putting the phone down, he said, "This Deamer business, it's starting to give me a headache. You promised me you'd have something on my desk by now." Reg wore classic sideburns, a beard and a creased off-white shirt signifying his earlier days as a pavement boy. He wore his black trousers handsomely, done up with a belt and fitted with black patent leather shoes. He could have been a school teacher.

"You also said you didn't want something that was half baked."

"God-dammit, we had Alan write a glowing review of Deamer's book, and now we've been made to look like fools!" Reg thumped his desk in anger, the papers jumping with the force.

"I'm not exactly sure who's the fool here."

"Don't test me Garret."

There were only a few journos on the floor that could stand up to Faraday. Garret was one of them, mainly because they went to the same school together, although about ten years apart. Sydney Boys High. And then the University of Sydney. Degrees in media communications.

"I always smelled a rat about that book," Garret said. "I tried to warn Alan, but he wouldn't listen. He loved it. Thought it painted a true picture of contemporary Sydney. Specially the cop part."

"Well it did, didn't it. What's changed?"

"Nothing I suppose."

Reg took stock of Garret. He liked him. But he thought he was too slow. He produced good work, except it was always late. If he could just put a fire-cracker up his arse ... "So where are we up to on this? How soon can you put something across my desk?"

"I'm trying to decide if I should put this fire out—or fan it. I haven't decided yet."

"Put it out."

"What happened to 'Bad News Is Good News'? I thought that was our mission statement."

"It is. But that was when no one gave a shit about Finn stealing Zac's idea. If you weren't so fucking slow, Parkinson wouldn't have gotten the jump on us, would he?"

"I prefer to be thorough."

"Thorough doesn't sell papers."

"Well what do you want me to do?"

"I want to you to fix it! Find out why Finn has vanished. Right now it's looking like Parkinson's theory is correct."

"What if it is?"

Faraday gave Garret a cock-eyed look. "You believe that horseshit?"

"I respect Bob as a journalist. He's got experience, he's got a good track record. When has he ever been wrong?"

Faraday mock-pretended to pull his hair out. It was short and wiry. Like his beard. He dropped his hands to his sides and gave them a slap. He was getting down to business. "So you think

Finn murdered Zac?"

"Doing a runner hasn't exactly polished his image, has it?"

"What if he didn't run? What if something happened to him?"

"Like what?"

"I donno. Maybe he was abducted by aliens! Who knows. He could have run off with the Mexican cartels."

"Or maybe he's gone underground, as a ploy, to cook up more publicity."

Faraday's eyes sparkled. "Yeah, I like that."

Garret shook his head. "You gotta be pulling my leg, right?"

Faraday threw his hands up in frustration. "Yes! I am pulling your leg. And if you don't give me something in the next 24 hours, I'm going to fucken pull your head off as well!"

"Ok, ok. I'm on to it." Garret got up to leave.

"One more thing ..."

Garret turned around. "What?"

"Don't tell Parko anything about this. I don't want him getting even the slightest whiff of this. You understand?"

"Sure."

"I need you to come good on this one Dick. This could be the story of the century."

Garret couldn't help chuckling. He opened the door and said, "Last time you said it was the story of year," and walked out.

– 3–
Ali Baba's
Cleveland Street

"You promised to call me."

Garret looked at Leila Sheshan with his best-mannered smile. He didn't want to put her off. He felt she could have been a butterfly, slip through his fingers, and he didn't want that. He needed to hear what she had to say. The problem was just getting it out of her.

"I'm sorry," she said, drying her hands off on her waitress' smock, "I can't talk right now. It's lunch hour."

"Ok, I'll have some lunch then," Garret said. All he had was a cup of coffee for breakfast. He could do with a bit of food in his stomach.

Leila didn't hide her disappointment. She showed him to a table at the back.

Ali Baba's had Persian frescoes on the walls, Formica tables and rubber cushioned chairs. Turkish tabla music quietly ran in the background. The air had a tinge of rose water to it. He took a table right at the front, so he could look outside to pass the time.

For quite a while, Leila ignored him and attended to other customers who were filtering in for lunch. Was she trying to get rid of him? If she was, it wasn't going to work. Garret, while not happy with the treatment, expected it as part of his job. He had developed a sort resigned patience to handle it.

When she finally came to his table, he ordered lamb kaftas and hummus. When she said, "Is that all?" he extemporized and said, "Ok, add the spinach rolls."

He didn't intend eating the spinach rolls, but she ignored him again until the restaurant emptied, and so he ate them to stave off boredom. They ended up tasting better than he expected and he began toying with the idea that he ought to improve his diet.

When she finally came back, she said, "I can't talk here. I have half an hour. We can talk in the park."

They walked to Prince Alfred Park, the sun was warm, the air nice and cool. Leila wore a shirt that covered her arms, and a pair of slacks with jelly sandals and white socks. Her hair was auburn, mostly straight and below shoulder length, but Garret suspected it was originally dark and she had dyed it. It was her eyebrows though, that attracted him the most. They were thick and strong and accented her beautiful almond eyes. There was an intelligence in those eyes, but also a wariness. He sensed she was tense and wanted to get this over as a formality as quickly as possible.

As they walked, he said, "I found out Zac got a diploma in creative writing as well as a degree in English Literature at the University of Sydney. He must have been serious about wanting to be a writer."

"He was. But not in the way that you might think."

"Oh, how so?"

"He didn't believe in the industrialization of fiction."

"Industrialization?"

"That's what he called it."

They entered the park, from the southern side. Walked past the tennis courts and sat down at a picnic bench next to the public barbecues.

Garret said, "I suppose I get the meaning of what he said. I tried my hand a creative writing while I was doing media studies. I was never any good at it so I switched to journalism. I get my words from other people, then all I to do is put them in the right order."

"Zac wouldn't have approved."

"I suppose not. Everything I've heard about him suggests that he was not one to compromise."

"No, he despised compromise."

"So what was your relationship with him, if you don't mind me asking?"

Leila thought about the question for a moment, steered her

eyes away to think. When she returned them to him, she said, "You can't publish any of this. You have to promise me."

"I won't publish anything you don't want me to."

Leila glanced at her fingernails, which were short and varnished with clear lacquer. "We weren't boyfriend and girlfriend, or anything like that. Our connection was intellectual. We both shared a love for stories. I used to tell him stories that my mum told me about Beirut. She described it as the 'Paris of the Middle East.' Because of that I've always had these romantic ideas about it, the art and the fashion. Zac said that's why I should become a writer. Because I have a love of art flowing through my veins."

"That's a nice story. Did he tell you anything about himself?"

"He called himself a wandering Jew. Disconnected from his homeland, his past, his family."

"Dispossessed."

"Something like that. The only thing he ever said was that his father used to be a poet in Moscow."

"Moscow?"

"Yeah, he's a Russian Jew. He was married to a Muscovite."

"I see."

"When he came out to Australia, he got a job working for a kosher butcher in Bondi. That was his original trade Zac said."

"A butcher poet."

Leila smiled for the first time since their meeting.

"So how did you first meet?"

"What, me and Zac?"

"Yeah."

"Zac worked part-time as a dish hand in my father's restaurant."

"Oh, I didn't know it was your father's."

"It's a family business." She looked at her watch.

Garret stalled her with another question. "There's one thing I don't understand. Why was Zac working as a dish hand? I mean ... he had the entire world at his feet. From what I heard, he topped his class. Got a high distinction."

"Where did you hear that?"

"I spoke to one of his lecturers at the university."

"Then you know more about him than I do."

"But I still don't understand, why he didn't use his degree to get a better job."

"Zac once told me that no one owned him, not even God."

"So he was fiercely independent."

"I felt like he preferred to be alone. He didn't like interacting with others, even in the kitchen. Although he liked to talk, my father kept a sharp eye on him, so he generally just came in, washed and took his money."

"But he talked to you."

"He encouraged me to pursue my dream of writing, yeah."

"Did he encourage you to go to university?"

"I was planning on going to university but my mother got sick and so I've taken over most of her responsibilities. It doesn't leave me with much energy at the end of the day. But hopefully one day in the future I'll get the opportunity to go."

"May I ask how old you are?"

"Twenty-two." She looked at her watch again. "I have to go." She stood up.

"I'll walk you back," he said.

They retraced the same path they took getting to the park, Garret asking her more questions as they went.

"I was wondering ... do you think you can tell me about the party? Finn Deamer's party at his parent's place in Point Piper."

They walked in silence for a while before Leila said, "What I can tell you is that I didn't stay the whole time. I left before midnight."

"Ok. But you saw Finn and Zac together?"

"Yes."

"And ... what can you tell me about what you saw."

They came out onto Chalmers Street and headed south towards Cleveland Street.

"All I can tell you is the same thing I told the police."

"Oh, so you've already spoken to the police?"

"Yes."

"Do you remember their names?"

"Of the police?"

"Yes."

"I think it was Detectives Phelps and Mooney."

"Right. I'll make a note of that. So what did you tell them?"

Leila's face grew a little tense. Garret sensed she didn't want to talk about it.

"Just the basic details," he said, encouraging her.

"There was some antagonism between them. Zac accused Finn of stealing his idea."

"Ok."

"The story, according to Zac, is that they were at the pub one day arguing about the merits of literary versus commercial fiction. Zac was saying anyone could come up with a commercial idea, all you needed was sex, money and murder."

Garret interjected, "Not necessarily in that order."

"No. So to prove his point Zac came up with a story called My Secret Disease."

"About a serial killer and his wife."

"Yeah, and as far as Zac was concerned, that was the end of that. But then he finds out that Finn published a novel using the exact same title and storyline—without asking for his permission."

"Right, so it's a copyright violation."

"I suppose, yeah. But I think what really rubbed Zac up the wrong way—according to Zac at least—was that Finn accused him of being an Indian giver."

"An Indian giver."

"Yeah, someone who—"

"—I know what an Indian giver is: someone who takes back the gift they've given someone. I think it refers to the Indians in the wild American west. They wanted their land back from the settlers after they gave it to them."

"It should be the other way around. The land the settlers stole off the Indians."

"Oh yeah, history is always written by the victors."

"Which is ironic, because Zac felt that the success of Finn's novel re-wrote their history. Finn got his name on it and Zac wanted it the other way around. When Zac told me that, I said, 'but Finn wrote it.' Zac said, 'yeah, but he should have written a preface detailing my contribution.'"

"I'll be honest with you. I read the book and while I thought it was good, I felt that someone was trying to pull the wool over my eyes. I'm not saying Finn didn't do a good job. He did. But all he gave Zac was a one-line acknowledgement."

"Zac said that was disrespectful. He should acknowledge that he appropriated the idea."

"How much are we talking about?"

"Every detail."

"Every detail?"

"That's what Zac told me."

Garret audibly sighed. "That's a big claim."

"It's what he said."

They were standing outside Ali Baba's. Leila wasn't going inside yet. She waited for Garret to finish the interview.

Garret said, "I think we've barely scratched the surface. Do you mind if we meet again?"

"I'd rather not."

"Why?"

"Because I feel like we'll never get to the truth. What do I know? And so whatever I say you'll twist around to suit your paper."

"What if I find something new? Will you want to hear it." Garret looked at her and saw a moment of doubt.

"I don't know." She momentarily chewed the cuticle on her thumb.

"I'll take that as a yes."

"I've got to go now. Remember your promise."

"Deal." He offered his hand.

Leila waited for some pedestrians to walk by, then briefly took it and ducked back into the restaurant.

– 4 –
Waverley Street
Randwick

GARRET drove his Ford Capri from Redfern to Randwick, thinking about his conversation with Leila as he went. She struck him as an intelligent girl, vivacious and almost certainly stubborn. He wouldn't want to be married to her; she'd probably put all kinds of demands on him. Not that he ever thought of marriage. He had an on-again, off-again girlfriend, Sharon, who worked in the advertising business. She described their relationship with one simple analogy: sex is like hunger; when you get hungry you eat. He didn't think she loved him, which kind of bothered him. But then again, he wasn't sure he completely loved her either. The word 'convenience' often cropped up in their conversations. He suspected she was seeing other guys, which kind of made him want to chase after her, hold on to her, which he also suspected she didn't like. So he was left with no choice but to fall back onto his old familiar routine. The resigned patience that he had so carefully cultivated.

At thirty-two, he began to feel the twinge of loneliness. Talking to new people all the time, his bread-and-butter, ought to have kept the lights on at home, but the lights were getting dim. He wondered how long he could keep it up. Whether he should change his career, or keep plugging on, he couldn't quite decide. There was no master plan. He lived from day-to-day. Story-to-story. If this was going to be the story of the century, then maybe this was the one he ought to go out on.

Or ... if it won an award, then maybe it could launch him into a senior position. Maybe even television. He glanced at himself in the rear-view mirror, swiped his hair back, and saw a young Jack Benny. All he needed was the talent. And if not the talent, then at least the story.

He felt he could have gotten a whole lot more out of Leila, but experience told him not to push it too hard on the first meeting. Trust was something that had to be built up. In the meantime, there were still other fish to fry.

Hence this trip to visit Zac's father.

The butcher poet.

He smiled thinking about that.

Josep Levin had a three-day growth, his eyes were sunken and he smelled of alcohol. He let Garret into his apartment which was cluttered with books stacked high along the corridor from the entrance way through into the lounge, where a coffee table was cluttered with dirty plates and more books and papers.

A nearly empty bottle of vodka lay on it side on top of a book, *The Fixer* by Bernard Malamud.

"What do want?" Josep demanded. He flayed his arms out haphazardly, pointing at nothing and everything.

"I suppose you can start by telling me something about yourself," Garret replied, standing amidst the mess. He looked around, hoping to find somewhere to sit.

Josep pushed a pile of papers off a foot stool and motioned Garret to take it.

"What do you want to know?" Josep said. "That I was a bad father? A bad husband? And now a drunk?"

Garret held his tongue, he wasn't going to take the bait.

Josep plonked himself down on the sofa in the only spot that wasn't crammed with stuff. He stared at the TV for a moment, the blank screen staring back at him accusingly.

Garret said, "Zac's girlfriend called you a 'butcher poet'. I couldn't help being intrigued by that."

"Yeah, I butcher words for a living," Josep said. He waved his hand at the room. "Can't you tell?"

"Some of the best writing came from cut and paste ideas," Garret said, playing along.

"I suppose you'd know," Josep said. "Being a journalist and all. Got to fit all those words into those tiny little boxes, right?"

Garret smiled in agreement. "That's the editor's job. I just make sure I keep to the right word count."

"That's right. It's not what you say, it's how many words you say it in."

"You sound like you have some experience with that."

"I've published the odd poem in the Australian Jewish News."

"In that case, we ought to consider ourselves colleagues." Garret held his hand out, extending it like an olive branch.

Josep eyed him suspiciously for a while, then took it and shook it. Letting go he said, "So you're a lover of poetry then?"

Garret said, "Yeah, although I love all literature."

"So you don't write poetry."

"No. Just news."

"So you're a hack." It wasn't a question, it was a statement.

Garret, being quick witted, took the opportunity to break the ice. "Yeah, I'm also a butcher of words."

Josep briefly smiled in response. He slapped his thighs and made to get up. "I should've asked you, do you want something to drink?"

"No thanks," Garret said, politely refusing. In truth he didn't fancy drinking out of anything seeing all the dirty dishes lying around.

"If you don't mind, I'll help myself," Josep said, pouring the last of his vodka into a cup. He took a gulp, leaned back and said, "So, you want me to tell you something truthful about myself?"

"Preferably, yes."

Josep gulped another mouthful of vodka. He wiped his lips with the back of his hand and said, "I came out to Australia in 1979, as *noshrim*. My wife and I originally lived in Moscow, but our lives there were unhappy, it was a constant struggle, doors constantly being shut in our faces, so when the Soviet policy changed in 1971, allowing soviet Jews to return to Israel, we took it and ran. We first went to Vienna, then Rome, and from Rome by ship to Melbourne."

"Oh, so you lived in Melbourne?"

"For the first few years, yes. Then I got a job working as a kosher butcher in Bondi, and so we moved up here."

Garret was afraid to ask about the wife. She was obviously not around.

Sensing Garret's uneasiness, Josep said, "My wife returned to Melbourne, to stay with her sister."

"Ok. So you brought Zac up by yourself?"

"Mostly."

"Well, I don't blame Zac for staying here in Sydney. The weather's better for starters."

"It's not the reason he stayed. He didn't approve of his mother having an affair."

"Oh. I see."

"He was a sensitive kid. He had a strong sense of morals and his own identity from a very early age."

"So your wife didn't remarry?"

"The guy dumped her."

"I see."

Josep stared at Garret for a while, to see if he really did understand.

"I mean, it must have been hard on Zac," Garret said.

"It was hard on both of us. But what can you do? Life doesn't take sides. It's indifferent to our suffering. We're just particles in a cosmic pinball machine."

"You believe that?"

"Whether I believe it or not, it makes no difference. It's what *happens*."

A silence fell between them. The light filtered in through faded curtains. A gentle breeze from an open window moved them ever so slightly. Garret felt a sense of claustrophobia. He wanted to get up and go outside. But his instinct told him to sit and wait.

"It's been what, a week now," he found himself saying, "since Zac's passing. I'm finding it difficult to understand what happened. It must be even harder for you."

Josep wrung his hands. "He was my only son. My everything. He had such promise."

"I suppose, it's worth asking, did he leave any writing behind?"

Josep's lit up for a brief moment and he looked around. "I've got some of his writing here somewhere." He got up and went down a short hallway to a door.

Garret followed him.

"This is Zac's room," he said standing in front of it. "I haven't dared go in there yet."

"You don't have to."

Josep opened the door and went in. The curtain was drawn. The bed was unmade, a doona half draped over the mattress onto the floor. A chair was overlaid with a pile of clothes. There was a bookshelf made from stacked boards and bricks. The titles were eclectic, ranging from literature to philosophy to science. Over on a desk in the corner was a typewriter—he recognized it as an Olivetti Lettera—its roller was empty but there was wastepaper basket next to the desk that was filled with balled-up pieces of paper. He was tempted to reach in and pull one out. But then his eye caught a notebook lying on a bedside table next to Dostoevsky's *Crime and Punishment*.

"May I?" he asked.

Josep didn't seem to hear him. He was just standing there, staring blankly into space.

Garret thought about it for a moment, then picked up the notebook and flipped it open. Therein he read:

Literary critics laud Crime and Punishment for its portrayal of a mind tortured by guilt. In reality, it is a superficial melodrama that has no connection with actual human behavior. Dostoevsky starts out by briefly presenting Raskolnikov, an aimless young man who is in debt. This is supposed to be sufficient motivation for mur-

der. He gives us the pivotal moment: "A strange idea had emerged in his head, like a baby chick pecking its way out of its egg, and it interested him greatly." The "idea" came after Raskolnikov sold his father's silver watch and gold ring to a pawnbroker (who happens to be a nasty old hag) and in return only received two "small notes" – the implication being that he got robbed by her. So the motivation appears to be revenge. The idea is further reinforced by a coincidental event: in a tavern, Raskolnikov overhears a young officer and a student whom he has never met talk about the pawnbroker in a disparaging way, saying that she is no more than a "cockroach" and that murdering her would actually "benefit" society.

The reader is supposed to believe that the combination of Raskolnikov's "idea" and the accidental overhearing of strangers condoning murder is sufficient motivation to commit the crime. Dostoevsky then shows Raskolnikov prepare for the murder: he invents an ingenious solution to carry an axe concealed in his coat, after which he steals the axe, rehearses the approach (he even has a dream of killing a horse with an axe), then he "mechanically" kills the old hag, and by way of fate, her half-sister as well, who happens to stumble in on the crime while he is committing it.

So we are shown motivation, preparation, and commission. On the surface, all of this would seem plausible.

But is it?

Dostoevsky wants us to believe that a person who has no prior history of violent behavior is able to leap directly to a double murder based purely on ideological motivation. Talk about fanciful!

Okay, so he is writing a fable. It doesn't have to be realistic. He is pursuing a different message. What is that message?

Dostoevsky spends the rest of the book showing us a character whose mind unravels under the weight of self-recrimination, causing him to eventually confess. So it is a fable about consciousness knowing the difference between right and wrong.

Unfortunately, he fails on this level as well.

The consciousness of premeditated murderers shares nothing in common with Dostoevsky depiction. These individuals do not agonize over their actions. Quite the opposite; they rationalize them—not as Dostoevsky would have us believe, by some inverted morality suggesting a benefit to society—but for its own ends, for self gratification. They do not leak psychological and behavioral clues of their guilt as Dostoevsky describes Raskolnikov doing on numerous occasions. Rather, they surgically compartmentalize the crime from their normal everyday lives. Their best friends notice nothing, suspect nothing. They do not fall into fits of delirium wondering whether it was a bad dream. They know exactly what they did. They don't get emotional over it because there is no emotion. There is, if anything, a feeling of superiority that they got away with it.

In other words, Dostoevsky has given us a character that doesn't exist in reality, and as a fable, it only appeals to those who are ignorant of how consciousness actually works.

Garret flicked through the journal to read some other entries, but his eyes stopped taking anything in, the impression of Zac's words created a white-out in his brain. A regular blizzard that almost made him lose sense of space and time. He closed the notebook and put it back where he found it. He slowly turned around and looked at Josep, who was still standing there, seemingly staring at nothing, his eyes unblinking.

"I think we've seen all that we need to see here," Garret said quietly.

Almost robotically, Josep closed the door behind them. Garret plodded his way through the lounge, down the corridor to the front entrance. Josep opened the door for him.

"Thanks for your time," Garret said.

The two men shook hands.

Garret took the stairs down to ground level and walked to his car, which was parked out front. He got in, turned the keys and started the engine. However he didn't drive off right away, he had to think about where he wanted to drive to, his mind still up there somewhere in Zac's room.

Eventually an idea came to him. It was time to visit Finn's editor. It was time to see just how much of Zac really went into that book.

– 5 –
Geraldo & Sons
Pitt Street, Sydney

GARRET was surprised that Finn's editor was a woman. Not that he had any preconceived notions ...

"Somehow Geraldo & Daughters doesn't have the same ring to it," Evelyn Harper said, crushing out a half-smoked cigarette in an already over-crowded ashtray. A dog-eared manuscript lay in front of her, separated into two piles, one with heavy red markings on it. A framed photograph of a much younger Evelyn with an author Garret didn't recognize hung crookedly on the wall. A book case with books and bundled manuscripts filled one side of the room. Garret tried to imagine what the younger Evelyn might have looked like. The woman he saw sitting in front of him seemed tired and grumpy, the carefully applied thick make-up barely concealing the worn edges.

"No, I guess not," Garret said, taking a chair.

"I suppose you want to know, along with every other man and his dog in this town, if I knew about Finn's theft of Zacharia Levin's idea before I signed him on?" She stared at Garret in a flippant manner that suggested she didn't care one way or the other what he thought. "If you want to know—the answer is ... sort of."

"Sort of?"

"I prefer the proverbial short story, but somehow I get the feeling you're going to keep biting my ankles until you get the long one, so here it is."

Garret settled himself into his chair in expectation.

"Where should I start?" Evelyn asked herself. She reached for a new cigarette, then thought the better of it. "Deamer came to me through an agent, which if you know, was set up by his mother, Veronica—she runs a small exhibition space in Waterloo—she's a high society woman, has more connections than a telephone exchange, and champions her son as the next F. Scott Fitzgerald—which he's not, mind you, and never will be—but that's beside the point, he came to me with this opening chapter. A single opening chapter. Yes! Highly recommended by his agent, blah blah blah, so I had no choice but to read it, and to my surprise, it was actually quite good. It hooked me in. So I called him up, I wanted to see the face and the hand that created it. Arranged a meeting right here in this office—"

"—When was this?"

"Let me see. December last year."

"About nine months ago."

"That'd be about right. It took about six months to knock the manuscript into shape. The type setting and cover art took another two months."

"That's pretty fast."

"I run a tight ship Mr. Garret. So where was I? Yes. The young Deamer steps into my office, and I literally cannot believe my eyes. The guy doesn't look anything like a writer. He was brought up with a silver spoon in his mouth for Christ's sake's. His clothes were too neat, his shoes too expensive. He spoke like a dandy."

"No!"

"I kid you not. 'How are your horses running today?' That kind of claptrap."

Garret laughed.

"You know his father, Errol Deamer, right?"

"Big hot shot banker?"

"That's the one."

"Exactly. So what do you think Daddy Deamer wants his son to do?"

"Wants him to follow in his father's footsteps, naturally."

"Naturally. So this pip-squeak Deamer is working as a junior clerk in a bank—" Evelyn snapped her fingers trying to recall, "—in customer service I believe, and he tells me he writes chapters in his lunch hour on the back of bank stationary, and low-and-behold, I see the letterhead on his manuscript, and it's Westpac!

Can you believe that? He's a regular John!"

"I wouldn't have put it past him."

"Ok, so there's your answer."

"So you suspected him right from the start."

"Wouldn't you?"

"I suppose so, based on what you've told me."

"Exactly. But anyway, I played along. Why not. It was a good opening. A bit racy, you know, but nothing that we couldn't get past the censors. And so we set up a schedule, and he duly went about churning through his bank's stationary like he was doing an extracurricular exercise. Brought in chapters to me each week."

"Right."

"But this is where things went a little pear-shaped. That lustrous diamond he brought in, yeah? He turned the bloody thing it into a lump of coal."

Garret found himself chuckling mirthlessly.

"So I did the only thing I knew how. I took the bull by the horns and educated him. Made him re-write each scene. Open a vein, that sort of thing. At first he resisted, but then he gradually got into it. Specifically, when I convinced him to get a fake doctor's certificate and take off sick from work. I can proudly say I was the one who introduced him to Whiskey sours."

"You like that drink?"

"Love it."

"Ok ..."

"Before my very eyes, he started transforming into a writer. He came in unkempt, bleary-eyed, wracked with anguish, and that's when the magic started happening."

"Wow!"

"Yeah. And this is where I'd like to say that I was the one who was responsible for turning that junket around. But then something happened. You see, I made him go into each murder, one by one, create a full background for each victim. Literally live in the victim's shoes. You know? And he took it to heart. He really went down the rabbit hole. And that's when I started seeing a change. He became quieter, almost too polite, but his eyes ... they sent shivers down my spine. I can still feel it now thinking about it." She shuddered like she was reliving it. "At that point, I thought, geez, maybe I've made a mistake here. I've corrupted a young boy. Any moment now his dad is going to walk in and shut me down."

"Did he?"

"He did come here once, to congratulate me when the book sales started taking off. But he also warned me. He said Finn was too young for success. It would ruin him. Lie to him about the actual sales figures he said. It was the only choice. It was his son, how could I refuse him?"

"No, you did the right thing."

"Except I can't get rid of that nagging feeling that I broke something inside him. What if I uncovered a part of his personality that led to ..."

Garret didn't want to say it.

Neither did Evelyn.

But it was in the air.

"The question you wanted answered, I think I gave you all you need to know," she said quietly. This time she didn't hesitate. She shakily reached for a cigarette and lit it up.

Garret didn't hold it against her. As he watched her, a mute sadness washed over him. What if she was right? How would that change things? Stories are tools for living he once heard someone say. He forgot who said it. But it seemed to him that stories could also be weapons of mass destruction. How many people of the world went to war over a story they believed—true or false, it mattered little.

And then he thought—but no one really takes stories seriously. Do they? There was no Thomas Wilford. He was a just character made up by a writer who didn't think twice about the consequences of what he made up. In all probability, it was just a game to him. An intellectual exercise to prove he was clever. Nothing more.

And yet ... look where they were now.

One dead young writer.

One missing young writer.

Which made him think: "It's been three days now since Finn has gone missing," he said. "Have you had any word from the police, or from anyone else?"

"No. I called the police this morning. Nothing. It's like he vanished into thin air."

"What about his parents? Do they have any idea where he might have gone?"

"His parents are not due back from Europe until tomorrow."

"Oh."

"His girlfriend—Nikki—she's minding the house. She's devastated of course."

"So I suppose she doesn't know anything either? I assume the police have interviewed her."

"She called me and told me they had. But she had nothing to offer."

"Nothing at all?"

"Nope. The only thing we talked about was Finn's new manuscript. It's lying unfinished on his desk."

"Really? I heard a rumour, but I didn't think it was true."

"It's true."

"So this Nikki ... perhaps she knows more than she letting on. Or perhaps the police have been asking her the wrong questions."

"I can't speak for her. All I know is she's devastated."

He dwelled on that information for a moment, acknowledged the unfortunate circumstances that brought it about, then reached into his pocket and pulled out a little notebook. "I have his address here somewhere," he said. He muttered to himself as he searched ... "Yeah, here it is: one sixty-four Wolseley Road, Point Piper."

"That's the one."

– 6 –

Woseley Road
Point Piper

EVELYN called the Deamer household, got Nikki on the phone, set up the interview. There was no way she would have done this while the theft of Zac's idea was still in the ether. She would have gone to any lengths to protect Finn, like a mother tiger protecting her cubs. But now that he was missing, she had no choice. If that meant getting into bed with a hack journalist, then so be it.

The drive took Garret up New South Head Road, giving him glimpses of the harbour as he went. The air was crisp and clear, etching the outlines of white sails and ferry wakes on the shimmering water. Apartment blocks and houses, many of them deluxe, crowded down to the rocky shores. People on the streets were smartly dressed, some of the them wearing chic combinations of designer labels. There was no mistaking it, this part of Sydney smelled of money. But his was just a taste of what was to come.

He took the turn off into Woseley Road, and at first he passed upper middle class properties and apartment blocks. But as he made his way to the point, the architecture changed and he was soon driving past some of the wealthiest real estate in the country.

He slowed down, searching for the house number. He counted them down till he bracketed the number he was looking for and found a nearby on-street parking spot and parked his car.

From the exterior, the house was quite discreet. It presented itself in the style of modern minimalism, with clean modular lines, and was low-lying, almost as if trying to flatten itself against the ground. The only sign that something extraordinary might lie behind its façade was the pair of large, dark wooden doors at its entrance. Garret approached and pressed the buzzer.

It took a while, but eventually they parted, and he found himself being greeted by a young woman. For an instant, he was struck by her uncanny resemblance to Modigliani's favorite muse, Jeanne Hébuterne. There was an unmistakable air of melancholia about her; the haunted eyes, the nervous hands ... under any other circumstance it ought to have weighed him down. Another weary interview. But no, he didn't feel that way at all. Rather, he felt an instant desire to be drawn into her world.

She ushered him inside and he walked down a spacious hallway, past framed photos of the Deamer family, a collection of African masks, and into a dining room adorned with a large Brett Whiteley depicting a sandy beach, blue water and birds of paradise. His eyes, however, were quickly drawn to the view of Sydney harbour, framed by the opened plantation shutters and spacious terracotta deck, and then to Nikki, as she glided out and stared at the scene.

He didn't say anything right away, he gazed at her, then at the view.

"I'm sorry, I should have offered you something to drink," she said after while. The French inflection instantly endeared him. She wasn't what he would call the perfect example of the 'French girl aesthetic,' but she did exude an effortless elegance with her simple buttoned-down blouse, cigarette pants, and Bali sandals. Her eyes were watercolor green and her hair a faded blond—she only partially tied it back leaving the rest to caress her cheeks.

"Thank-you. Mineral water if you have it," he said, realizing that his throat was parched.

She went into the kitchen through an alternate doorway and came back with a tall glass for himself, and a glass of white wine for herself.

"Thanks."

She took a sip of her wine and stared jointly at the view with him.

"It's the only thing that's been keeping me sane," she said. "Watching the boats go by, seeing the different conditions each day."

"It's sort of mesmerizing, I gotta admit," he said, after nearly downing half his drink.

"You must have been thirsty. Do you want me to get you another one?"

"Hmmm ... maybe. Let me see how I go with this one."

"Ok."

A moment of silence fell between them, then Garret said, "I suppose, you wouldn't be able to tell me about your relationship with Finn, would you?"

"That would depend on which parts you want to talk about, wouldn't it?"

"If you put it like that, I guess so. You can always decline, if you don't like my questions."

"Let's see. Why don't we sit down?"

There was a pair of cane chairs with outdoor pillows. Nikki took one, Garret the other. He was surprised that he still had a good view over the green hedge that fringed the harbour-side boundary of the property. The pool on the terrace below was a brilliant aquamarine blue, it made him feel like he was at an exclusive resort.

"Lovely, isn't it?" Nikki said, taking another sip of her wine. She swilled it, watching the motion of the liquid as it swirled around.

"It is. Now I know what Finn's editor meant when she said he grew up with a silver spoon."

"You're jealous."

"Shit yeah I am."

Nikki laughed. A soft, courteous giggle.

"I suppose wealth is relative, when you get used to it," he mused.

"I never get used to it. My parents were poor. I'm a working-class girl."

"You could have fooled me."

"No it's true. That's what Finn liked about me. He said I reminded him of his mother. Apparently she also came from a working class family."

"What about Deamer. Errol Deamer?"

"To be honest, I don't know much about him. He keeps his cards close to his chest as they say."

"Your English is quite good," Garret said, trying to be genuine.

"Are you teasing me?" Nikki said, leveling her gaze at him. She was serious.

"No! Not at all. I mean it."

Nikki leaned back, relaxed a little. "Then I'll take that as a compliment."

"Please do."

"You may think I fit in here, how do they say—'hand in glove'—but I can assure you, it's hard work. I spent all morning in bed. I couldn't get out I was so depressed."

"Really?"

"Yeah."

"Is that because of Finn's disappearance?"

"Partly."

"I see. So it's the whole thing?"

"The relentless pressure, being on call, the photo shoots, the expectation that I am supposed to be the right person for Finn ..."

"Are you the right person for him?"

She looked at him with a practiced gaze, like she had been through this a thousand times. "I don't give a fuck what people think about me and Finn."

The vulgarity momentarily hung in the air.

"Fair enough. It matters little to me. It's the people in the industry that you have to worry about. I have to deal with the same shit."

"As a journalist?"

"Yeah, as a journalist. The waters are shark infested, believe me."

"So Finn told me."

He looked at her. It took a moment for him to catch on. He took another sip of his mineral water. "Tell me," he said, "where did you guys first meet?"

"Oh, that? Yeah, we met at his book signing in Dymocks." She laughed freely.

"So you were a fan?"

"No, not at all! I just happened to be walking by. I had just arrived from Paris. There was a big crowd, I went inside to see what was going on. Then I saw him."

"I see. Love at first sight!"

"No! Nothing like that." She waved the idea away.

"Then what was it?"

"I listened to him read and I liked what I heard. So I hung around a bit. He noticed me, and I introduced myself."

Garret made a mental calculation in his head. *So that was less than a month ago ...* "And I guess, the rest is history, as they say."

"It all happened so fast. Like I was caught up in a ... what do you call it? A tornado?"

"A whirlwind."

"Yeah. A whirlwind."

"So when did Zac come into the picture?"

Nikki nodded, like she expected the question. "Strange, it was on the same day."

"Really?"

"Yeah. I know. Finn took me to the Light Brigade Hotel, for drinks. We talked. He asked me about my career. I told him I came to Sydney on a modeling contract. He told me he worked as a banker, but now that his book was published and seemed to be attracting a lot of attention, he was thinking that maybe he ought to quit. It was just telling his father about it that worried him."

"Oh yeah, I can see that."

"But his book was really going well, you know. And so I said, quit! Follow your dream!"

"He must have liked that."

"I think it scared him more than anything."

"You mean he was scared of daddy. The big powerful banker who could squash him like a fly if he wanted."

"That's it. Mr. Deamer wouldn't be happy I'm sure, unless Finn's book sold in the millions, and even then he'd question the value of it."

"Finn told you that?"

"In so many words. From what I have seen though, he takes more after his mother than his father."

"You've met his parents?"

"No, I've only talked to Mr. Deamer on the phone, briefly. They're still in Europe. No—actually, they're on their way home right now. They arrive tomorrow morning."

"Where from?"

"London."

"They'll be tired."

"Yes. But they will probably talk to police as soon as they get here."

"Oh, yeah, the police. I heard you talked to them. I suppose you told them pretty much the same thing you're telling me?"

"Pretty much. They wanted to know about the party."

"Of course, the party. I was going to ask about that."

Nikki took another sip of her wine and put it down on the side table between them. "Everyone wants to know what happened at the party."

"So are you going to tell me?"

She summed him up for a moment, then smiled. "Why not. What can I say that you don't already know? After all, it's been in the news non-stop since Zac's body was found."

"Maybe you'll remember something that you haven't told anyone before."

"Yes, like after drinking wine, I might be drunk enough to say things that I shouldn't."

Garret cocked an eye at her. "So there are some things that you haven't talked about—yet?"

"Maybe." She was teasing him.

He smiled. "Well I'm all ears." He finished his drink in anticipation.

"Do you want me to get you another one?"

"I wouldn't mind. Say, is it okay if I borrow the bathroom?"

She got up and pointed the way. "Take the corridor off the dining room, go down the stairs. You'll find it down there."

"No worries."

He walked into what looked like a separate apartment. Judging by the pictures on the walls and the clothes strewn about, this must be Finn's living quarters. He found the bathroom and relieved himself. Afterwards, he washed his hands, checking out his demeanor in the mirror. This time, he thought he was too old. She was too young. What chance did he have? He only wanted her to like him. He dried himself off on a plush towel. Went back out and stopped. She was standing there with his drink in her hand, another glass of wine in the other. She startled him. Right then and there he thought she was one of the most beautiful women he had ever seen up close in real life.

"Sorry," she said. "I didn't mean to scare you."

He smiled his best smile. "I'll survive."

She handed him his glass. He took a sip. "So this is Finn's castle I presume?"

"Yes."

"And where does that lead?" he asked, pointing to a side door.

"The laundry."

"Oh."

"The laundry leads to small courtyard, and from there to a door and a narrow side path down to Lady Martin Beach."

"Really?"

"You wanna see?"

"Yeah."

He followed her through the laundry into the courtyard. She showed him the door. She opened it, and they went out onto the narrow side path. From the outside, the door had a combination lock, a mechanical key pad. It occurred to Garret that this must have been the way that Zac found his way to the water, because Lady Martin Beach was just down the end of the path. They walked to the water, the waves lapped up onto the sand right there. The house literally abutted onto the harbour.

"Wow!" was all he could say.

"Yeah, pretty good, isn't it?"

"Must be worth a fortune."

"Finn said the house cost his dad about ten million when he first bought it. He said they then spent another two million renovating it afterwards."

"It must be worth close to fifteen or more now," Garret guessed.

They were looking at the property from the back. Garret saw the reason why it had such a low profile from the front. It was built into the hill.

They walked back up the path, Nikki punched in the key code. They walked back through the laundry, back through Finn's room and back up to the main level.

Garret laughed, because he just realized they had carried their glasses all the way.

"Like 'haute culture,'" Nikki said, striking a pose.

"So this is what the party was like," he asked. "Beautiful people, lots of expensive alcohol—"

"—and cocaine," Nikki added mischievously.

"I was about to say that."

"We all enjoyed it—except Leila, you know, Zac's girlfriend. Which I thought was strange, considering that it was her brother who supplied it."

"Really?"

"Yeah, but it's not what you think. Leila had nothing to do with it."

"So that explains why she didn't partake."

"Partake?"

"Use."

"Oh."

"So you're saying she didn't know her brother supplied the cocaine, or she did know, but didn't get involved?"

"It was Zac who organized it."

"Ha?"

"I know. Let me explain."

Garret let her know he was most interested to hear what she had to say.

"We're back at the Light Brigade Hotel again," she said.

"With Finn?"

"Yes. And guess who turned up?"

"Don't tell me, Zac?"

"Oh, so you know?"

"No, I was just guessing, from what you said."

Nikki expressed surprise. "Ok, so yeah, so Finn and I were talking, Finn was telling me the story about how he got the idea to *My Secret Disease*. He didn't lie. He told me straight up it was Zac's idea."

"And you weren't disappointed?"

"No. Why?"

"Because it wasn't his idea."

"Why should that matter? All art is theft anyway. I don't believe in original ideas. No one owns anything."

"What about copyright?"

"Oh, that's not what I meant. Of course you still have to copyright your version of what you produce."

"Ok. So Finn admitted to stealing Zac's idea."

"Yes. But then, speak of the devil, at that very moment, Zac appeared. I didn't know who he was. He didn't introduce himself. He just stood there and stared at Finn with a very angry expression."

"No shit."

"Ha! No shit! I thought they were going to get into a big fight. But Finn was very nice and introduced me. Zac introduced himself. The very first thing Zac said was: 'You realize this guy is a liar and a thief?' And I said, 'You mean he stole your idea which you stole from someone else?' From that moment on, he looked at me like I was Finn's co-conspirator. You know what I mean? I thought, you know, I've made another enemy."

"It's not hard to make enemies these days."

"Maybe, but then he surprised me. He sat down and the two of them discussed what happened. Each gave his own interpretation. I listened, and in the end, I couldn't tell who belonged to the truth. Because they disagreed on so many points."

"Did they agree on anything?"

"Not really. Finn said 'an idea is just an idea.' He quoted his editor as proof. Saying something like, 'ideas are worth a penny, it's the execution that counts.'"

"What did Zac say to that?"

"He didn't disagree. But he said that his idea contained the seeds of its own execution. It was all in the original story. So there was only one way to tell it."

"He might have a point there."

Nikki shrugged. "Finn said there were too many variables, you couldn't predict in advance where it was going to go. Not the story, but the details. From one sentence to the next, he didn't know what he was going to write. And then his editor made him rewrite it anyway, so the editor was just as much to blame as he was."

"I see. It's not as simple as it looks."

"No. Because, and I believe this—some ideas already exist before us. You know what I mean? They exist in the universe. All we do is discover them. We are just the messengers."

"That may be true ..."

"And each word we choose, it's a new idea. It even comes down to punctuation."

Garret couldn't help beaming a smile.

"What?"

"I was thinking of Oscar Wilde." He took a moment to recall the story. "There was this guy, you see, who didn't think much of writers. Thought they were lazy slobs, parasites on society, that sort of thing. Wilde seemed to exemplify this picture and he asked him what he did all day—you know, implying that he didn't do anything. And Wilde, true to his form, said, Well, I spent the whole morning taking a comma out, then I spent the afternoon putting it back in again."

"You see! That's what I told you!"

Garret laughed heartily. He couldn't help liking this girl. She was so free spirited.

"Oh my, Finn was struggling hard with his new novel. Sometimes I thought that's exactly what he was doing, taking commas out and putting them back in again."

"That's what his editor said. He was working on a new novel. May I ask what it is about?"

Nikki took a moment to think about it. She seemed to be debating with herself how much she ought to say. Eventually she said: "It's a story of redemption."

"He told you that?"

Nikki nodded.

"Let me guess, for stealing Zac's idea?"

Nikki nodded again.

"I see."

"But it's not what you think. He's not making it easy for the reader, or for himself. It's not like a confession or anything like that."

"I'm sure it isn't. If it was, Zac wouldn't have believed it."

"No. Yeah. Oh, I forgot to mention. After they finished their argument—"

"—After they agreed to disagree—"

"—Yeah, after they agreed to disagree, I said to Zac, why don't you come to Finn's post-publication party?"

"Ah, I see."

"Yeah, I thought, these two boys could do with some partying, to get the bad vibes out of their systems, you know?"

"So the party was your idea?"

"No, no!" She shook her head vigorously. "It was Finn's idea, he wanted to get his writing group together and celebrate. I just thought it would be nice if Zac came along and they made up."

"Right. Did Zac agree?"

"Sort of, yeah. He was hesitant at first. But he gradually warmed up to the idea."

"Ok."

"And that's when Finn asked him if he knew where he could get some coke, you know? And Zac said, yeah, he could get some. So Finn gave Zac, like, three hundred dollars."

"Right there?"

"Yeah. He did it discretely. Under the table."

"I see. So Zac came through with the drugs?"

"Sure did. And it was one hell of a party!"

"Must have been. But it makes me wonder ..."

"About what?"

"Zac coming through with the drugs like that. It sounds like he's done it before."

"Maybe. I don't know. But what I can tell you is Finn and Zac got into a fight afterwards. Zac threatened to go to the newspapers and 'spill the beans.' Ruin Finn's reputation. They were literally at each other's throat. I managed to get between them and pull Finn away."

"Sounds serious."

"It was."

"Later, I found Zac by himself. We got talking. We did some more lines of coke. Right? And one thing led to another."

"What are you saying?"

Nikki hesitated for a moment. "I didn't tell the police about this part. You have to promise me it's just between you and me."

"Sure."

"You promise you promise?"

"I promise."

Nikki considered Garret's sincerity for a moment. "The thing is, to my surprise, Zac and I sort of got on. I felt he was more creative than Finn. Maybe not as disciplined, but I was attracted to his mind. We talked about all sorts of things, and we danced together."

"Oh."

"Yeah. And I think it made Finn jealous."

"I'm sure it did."

"Actually, we kissed."

"What?"

"It wasn't anything serious. The coke probably got to our heads. But it is what it is."

"I'm not sure what I'm supposed to say ..."

"Finn never saw us. But ..." she trailed off.

"What?"

"Leila must have seen us and she stormed off. Left the party."

"When was this?"

"I don't know. Maybe around midnight. I'm not sure."

Garret's mind starting working overtime. "So when was the last time you saw Zac?"

"Maybe a little later. We broke off as soon as Leila saw us. Zac went out and tried to convince Leila to stay. Finn suspected something was going on. He went out and followed them. After that, I never saw Zac again. I didn't see Finn again for a while either, until I found him downstairs. He had changed his clothes, said he had spilled some beer on himself. I didn't press the matter any further."

"Until they found Zac's body floating in Rose Bay the next day."

"Pretty much."

"Did you confront Finn about it?"

"I did and I didn't. What could I have said?"

"Ask him if he had anything to do with it."

"I did sort of ask him that."

"And? What did he say?"

"He said I was stupid to ask. Of course he had nothing to do with it. He said the person I should really be speaking to is Leila. She was the last person to see him alive."

"Do you believe that?"

"I don't know what to believe."

Garret ran his hands through his hair, letting out a big sigh. "I suppose," he said, "the police have their own theory."

"If they did, they didn't tell me."

"I'm just wondering what they would have thought if you told them what you told me."

Nikki's face darkened. "You promised not to tell anyone what I told you."

Garret reached out and put a hand on her arm. "Don't worry. Your secret is safe with me."

Nikki searched his eyes.

Garret said, softly, "I do appreciate you sharing your story. I won't let you down."

She seemed to accept his sincerity.

A moment of silence passed between them. Then Nikki said, "Whatever Finn did, or didn't do, I'm worried about him. He always told me where he was going and when he would be back. He's been gone three days now ..."

"I know." Garret let his gaze return to the harbour, as if the answer lay out there somewhere.

Nikki comforted herself by wrapping her arms around herself.

Garret noticed and wondered, should he give her a reassuring hug? It seemed inappropriate. They had only just met. But she seemed so vulnerable. He felt at a loss. He decided to do the only thing that made sense. Leave, before things started getting murky. He made a very subtle motion towards the front entrance, then stalled.

Nikki picked up on it and unwrapped her arms. "Perhaps we should end it here," she said.

Garret nodded. He thanked her for the drink.

She reversed the French greeting on the way out.

Afterwards, as he drove back up the hill to the top of Woseley Road, he pulled over and idled the engine. The sensation of her cheek against his had lingered on his skin. He put his hand up to spot where they had made contact and caressed it. What was this world he had plunged into? It seemed both familiar and strange. Familiar because the whole thing seemed to hinge on words and stories. That excited him. Strange because he felt like he had become an accomplice to some dark deed. What, he could not exactly say. He had broken his golden rule; he was letting this become personal.

- 7 -
The Rose Hotel Chippendale
Cnr Cleveland & Shepherd

IT was time to talk to Detectives Phelps and Mooney. Reg Faraday, who had a direct line to the Police Commissioner, tipped him off as to their whereabouts. Garret found them drinking Toohey's New in the "back bar" of the Rose, two schooners a piece already downed, and onto their third. Garret braced himself, knowing he'd have to keep pace with their drinking to get anything out of them. He parked his car on Arundel Street, across from the University of Sydney, planning to retrieve it the next morning after taking a taxi home.

Homicide Detectives Ian Phelps and Dave Mooney couldn't have cut a more contrasting image; Phelps was tall and thin, Mooney, short and large around the waist. They were both in their early 40s, the first signs of grey hair streaking their sideburns.

"What brings you to our office?" Mooney said, as Garret sided up to them with a schooner in hand.

"Just doin' the rounds mate," Garret said, pulling up a bar stool.

"Like a regular dog looking for a tree to piss on," Phelps said.

"Well, I've always been partial to a good watering hole," Garret quipped, taking a swig from his schooner. "Figured you boys might have some interesting to share. Maybe something about a missing writer."

Phelps and Mooney looked at each other. An unspoken code passed between them.

Garret waited for them to finish their silent conference.

"I'll preface what I'm going to say with our standard disclaimer," Phelps said. "We can't release anything to the public that might jeopardize the case. What are you looking to find out?"

"Maybe we could swap notes," Garret offered. "I've learned a few things today that might interest you."

The detectives hitched their eyebrows with characteristic skepticism.

"Although I'm gonna have to preface what I say with my standard disclaimer," Garret added.

"Shut the fuck up," Mooney said, laughing into his glass.

Garret grinned like an idiot.

Phelps said, "What exactly did you learn today?"

Garret had prepared what he was going to say on his walk across the university campus. He felt he ought to be loyal to Nikki. He decided he would keep her secret—for now. Instead, he thought he might get a rise out of the detectives by speculating on what he thought had happened between Finn and Zac outside the house. "I had a good look at Lady Martin Beach, and I think that's where the murder occurred," he said, looking at each of them in turn.

"Who said it was a murder?" Mooney said.

"Very funny," Garret said.

"If you said 'alleged murder,' then we might have gone along with you," Mooney reminded him.

"Ok then, I think the alleged murder occurred down by the water. The way I see it, Finn had a motive to silence Zac after he threatened to go public with the true story."

The two detectives looked at each other.

Garret felt pleased with himself. So they only had their speculations to go on.

Phelps said, "So you weaseled your way into the Deamer house and interviewed Miss Sorbonne."

"Your powers of deduction are impressive," Garret said, taking a hefty swig of his beer.

"And she told you that Zac threatened Finn?" Phelps said.

"In so many words, yes."

"So you're prepared to go up against Errol Deamer on this?" Mooney asked.

Garret considered this. It had not slipped his mind that Errol Deamer was a powerful man and would do anything to clear his son of any 'allegations.' He would no doubt hire the best lawyers in the country. At the very worst, Finn would get off with manslaughter. More probably misadventure. But he didn't care about that. What he cared about was the truth. And above that, the story. "If you're asking, do I want to get my paper sued, no," Garret said. "In any case, it's not for me to decide. All I want is the story."

"The 'true' story," Phelps said.

"Yeah," Garret taking another swig of his beer. He was almost empty. He felt good, it hadn't gone to his head yet.

"Let's put it this way," Phelps said, "The autopsy wasn't exactly flattering. But this is just between you and us."

"Really?"

The detectives looked at their empty glasses.

Garret got the message. "My shout," he said, and went off to the main bar. He figured that by the time he got to the third round, anything beyond that would be diminishing returns. At least he hoped so.

After handing them their beer, Garret said, "You were talking about the autopsy ..."

"Were we?" Phelps said, feigning ignorance.

Garret was stymied. He took a long haul of his beer and decided to change tack. "Well .. let me tell what I learned about Zac, in person at least, if not body."

"Sure," Phelps said.

Mooney just took a swig of his beer and waited.

"My impression of Zac," Garret said, "is that he was too clever for his own good. I wouldn't go so far as to call him a misanthrope, but I don't think he ever got that close to people, even though he might have had numerous acquaintances."

"That he did have," Mooney confirmed.

"Ok, so I guessed right."

"Let's put it this way," Mooney said, "the DEA had him on their books."

"Ha?"

"Why do you think he skipped up north for six months?"

"Oh? So you're saying ..."

Phelps said it for him: "He was suspected of supplying cocaine to the night set in Bondi. His job as a dish-hand at Ali Baba's was just a front, we think."

Garret's eyes widened.

"There's a rumour that Ali Baba was on the laugh. It's only a rumour. But if true, he probably got spooked and decided to take a vacation," Phelps said, and then added, "But hey, we're only alleging this. None of this goes into print, right?"

"Of course," Garret said. He took a moment to process what he just heard, taking a long sip of his beer. "So where did he go?" he asked putting his glass back down.

"We're not sure. We think Darwin," Mooney said.

Garret started nodding to himself.

"What?" Phelps asked.

"I think I understand now. How Finn managed to steal Zac's idea without Zac knowing about it. To put it simply, when the cat's away, the mice will play."

"Except now the cat's out of the bag, we're all scratching our heads," Mooney chuckled.

"Maybe not quite," Garret said, playing on the moment.

The two detectives gave Garret a half serious look.

Garret let the moment hang a little longer.

"You wanna play the village idiot, or do you want someone to stroke your cock," Phelps said, forcing Garret's hand.

Garret laughed weakly. Then straightened up. "I did a little digging around," he said at last. "Found an old newspaper article. A school stabbing."

"And?" Phelps prodded.

"The perpetrator wasn't named, he was too young. But after a little more research I discovered the case was settled out of court. Guess whose name came up?"

"Santa Clause," Mooney said, not biting.

"Deamer," Garret said.

The two detectives did that thing again, where they looked at each other.

Garret said, "Interesting, don't you think?"

Phelps said, "How serious was it?"

"It didn't specify. I think the victim was briefly hospitalized."

"Was was the motive?"

"It was reported as an accident."

"An accident?" Mooney said.

"The article didn't specify. There was a brief flurry of articles about parental responsibility, tougher laws on kids who bring dangerous weapons into schools, that sort of thing, but it pretty much fizzled out."

"Okay Sherlock, you've got our attention," Phelps said. "You said you had a theory about what happened between Finn and Zac. Let's hear it."

Garret took a sip of his beer while gathering up his thoughts. "We take it as a given that Miss Sheshan left the party around midnight. Right?"

The detectives nodded in unison.

"What I propose is Zac went out there to find out why she was leaving, maybe they had an argument." He looked at the detectives to see their response. They were stone-faced. Ploughing on, he said, "So instead of going back inside right away, he goes down to the water, to cool off, so to speak. Meanwhile, Finn followed him out there. He hasn't planned anything yet, he hasn't got an idea what he's doing really, except that he wants to confront Zac again about his threat. He wants to convince Zac to change his mind. Ok?"

Phelps shrugged. "Go on."

"They get into another heated debate. Accusations fly. They're both intoxicated, mind you. And Finn snaps. He pushes Zac into the water. They get into a physical fight. It gets serious. Each tries to hold the other under water. Finn eventually comes out on top. He holds Zac under water long enough for him to lose consciousness. Finn, shocked at what he has done, pushes Zac out into deeper water. He goes back inside and changes. When people remark that he's wearing different clothes, he says he spilt red wine on himself, or something like that."

At first the detectives didn't say anything. They drained the rest of their beers.

"Well, what do you think?"

"I think you had better stick to journalism," Mooney said, speaking up first.

Phelps laughed.

Garret wasn't impressed. "What, why? I gave you a good theory."

"How do we know Miss Sheshan wasn't involved?" Mooney said.

Garret scoffed. "You're joking, right?"

"Or what about her brother, Dano? Fucken' Lebo thug," Phelps said.

Garret let out an exasperated sigh. "You're messing with me. I don't have to listen to this bullshit."

"The point being," Phelps said, "is that none of us are in a position to make a determination on this. Certainly not until Finn shows up."

"Or someone finds him," Mooney added.

Garret downed the last dregs of his beer. "Gentlemen, I think this meeting is over." He stood up.

"You're not going to have another one?" Mooney challenged.

Garret shook his head. "Some of us have to work tomorrow."

The detectives laughed. Raised their glasses and said, "Fucken' A grader!"

– 8 –
Bondi Beach

"To know the pain of too much tenderness."

Khalil Gibran — *The Prophet*

Zac parked his beat-up white Datsun 120Y in front of a heritage Victorian terrace on Wellington Street, Waterloo, and waited for Leila to come out. It was late August and the weather was just warming up again. The sycamores were regaining their leaves and the fuzzy balls that dropped in Autumn were reappearing as spiky green nuggets. The sun filtered through the leaves and cast dappled shadows on the pavement. It was a relaxing Sunday morning.

Leila came bounding out, full of energy and beaming a girlish smile. She wore baggy, faded blue jeans with a tan leather belt, sock-less Dunlop volley trainers, and a white tank top beneath a plain-woven light woolen jumper. A small, single-strapped handbag was slung over her shoulder.

"You're wearing a cross," Zac said, surprised. Indeed, a small crucifix dangled from a silver chain around her neck.

Leila tucked it away. "Yeah. It's just a memento." She placed her handbag on her lap and fastened her seat belt.

Zac took a moment to think about that, then started the engine. He was wearing his favorite printed T-shirt, jeans and Nike sneakers. A stenciled Gregor Samsor with the words: 'I woke up like this,' took pride of place across his chest. His thick, dark curly hair framed his high forehead and prominent nose. "I was thinking Bondi ... you wanna head down and see if we can get something to eat, then sit down somewhere and check out the scene?"

"Sounds good," Leila said, clasping her handbag with nervous excitement.

Zac headed up Foveaux Street and down Moore Park Road. "What do you feel like eating?" he asked as he negotiated the traffic.

"Fish and chips!" Leila said. "It's been ages since I had them."

"Fish and chips it is then."

Leila nodded enthusiastically.

"Did your father give you any grief for taking the day off?" he asked tentatively.

"No. My cousin is covering for me. She needed the pocket money, so there was no argument."

"Family business."

"Big family! My God, don't get me started."

"Same here."

Leila giggled. She unclasped her hands from her handbag and placed them on top in a more relaxed manner.

Zac felt himself relax a little as well. For some time now, he sensed that Leila was aware of the growing attraction between them, but small details in her behavior told him that this was less important than her much bigger goal of becoming a genuine artist. Like the way she diligently applied herself to writing tasks that she set for herself, oftentimes triggered by his critiques of other authors' works. He could tell, what she wanted, more than anything, was an honest appraisal of her writing ability. Despite her obvious talent, raw and instinctive as it was, she needed guidance, and it was he—Zac Levin—who she had chosen as her guide through the literary wilderness, so-to-speak, to help her find her true potential.

If only she had known that Zac harbored similar doubts himself. Although he had more experience as a writer, he still wasn't sure what the future held. Success and failure were both possible outcomes. He struggled to find the right words to express these uncertainties to Leila. In the end, he decided to say something simpler, hoping it would bring them closer together.

"You realize," he said, as he drove down Oxford Street, "that we're both first generation progeny of immigrants?"

"Don't tell me. My father reminds me every day! Ha!" She reflected for a moment. "Don't get me wrong. I love Lebanon. It's beautiful ... and tragic. My parents got out of there just in time, in 1976, at the start of the civil war. It was terrible. They had to sell *all* their possessions. Their house, their car, their plot of land on the slopes of Mount Lebanon. They sacrificed everything."

"Only to start over here with nothing."

"Yeah. And I don't take that for granted. My father is the hardest working person I know. And so is my mother. But sometimes I can't help feeling that what they're really doing is running away from something. They're putting all this time and effort into running the family business—"

"—Of course they are. Because they want you to take it over when they're gone."

"I understand that, but they've never once asked me what I want to do. They just assume that I'll follow in their footsteps."

"I'm lucky my father never ran his own business, so I've never had to deal with that."

"Do you think that allowed you to be free to explore your own ..." she searched for the word.

Zac helped her. "As the wise bard once said: Follow your Bliss."

"Follow your bliss. I like that."

"It's been my mantra—"

"—who said it?"

"Joseph Campbell."

Leila gave him a blank look, like she didn't know.

"Campbell was a mythologist. Wrote *The Hero with a Thousand Faces*. Hollywood swears by it. Which is why I feel a little squeamish when I mention it."

"That's right, I forgot. If it's Hollywood, it can't be good."

Zac flashed a glance at her. "Not necessarily. But generally, yes."

"Name a Hollywood film that you admire."

"*Casablanca*."

"That doesn't count. Everyone loves that."

"Ok, you got me there. How about the original *King Kong*."

Leila laughed. "Who would've thought a big hairy ape could be a star."

"Just don't say *The Sound of Music*."

Leila turned to him fully. "I love that movie!"

Zac slapped his forehead. "I bet you've still got all your ABBA paraphernalia too!"

"Yeah, I do!" She laughed at herself.

"I can't argue with the songs. I'm not a musician. But don't try to convince me that *The Sound of Music* is great art."

"Why not? It has some memorable songs. And the children were adorable."

Zac took pause for a moment. "So you love children?"

"I wouldn't say that I'm 'clucky.' I don't go 'goo-goo' every time I see a baby. But yes, I do want to have children—eventually."

"You sure of that?"

"I suppose so ... as much as I might gripe against my own family, I believe in it. My life wouldn't mean anything without it."

Zac started shaking his head.

"What?"

"So which is it? You love your family but you want your freedom ..."

Leila frowned. "You want to say I'm confused?"

"No." He turned off Oxford Street and took Old South Head Road."

"So what are you saying?"

"I'm saying ... I'm not saying I'm perfect. Far from it. As a writer you have to embrace your contradictions." He gave her time to digest that. "I don't want you to think that I'm attacking you. But you seem to think you can do both. You know? I mean, most of the great writers are men, right?" He looked at her to see her reaction. Her face momentarily pinched, then she pursed her lips. "I'm not saying there aren't any great women writers. There are. But they have to make one heck of a sacrifice to achieve it—far more than men do—just to, you know—"

"—Be great."

"Yeah, great."

"So you think it's tougher for women to be great?"

"I'm only telling you what I know. I'm talking about writers."

"I suppose if you count Mary Shelley, Virginia Woolf, Sylvia Plath ..."

"Don't forget Molinard."

"Never heard of her.

"She tore up everything she wrote until her husband one day managed to convince her to publish one of her manuscripts."

"What was it about?"

"Violence, mental illness ... the misogynist world she lived in."

Leila took a moment to absorb that. "It's not a good track record, is it?"

"And you think you can avoid it?"

The first glimpse of the ocean came into view. They momentarily stared at it. A circuit breaker.

He parked the car right on the water on Queen Elizabeth Drive. They got out and headed for Campbell Parade. They strolled through Bondi Pavilion on the way, looked at an exhibition of school children's art, naive, primary colors, family themes, read graffiti on the break wall 'Bondi Chicks Go Off', crossed Campbell Parade and started wandering south, Zac giving Leila a running commentary on his version of Bondi history.

Pointing up Beach Road, he said, "That used to be the Regis. I've seen some great bands up there. Joe Camilleri, INXS, Aussie Crawl, Hunters & Collectors ... we'd go in there and get blotto. Drink to destruction." He grinned at his own stupidity. "Not any more though. The new licensing laws have put a stop to it. It's all about pokie machines and quiz nights now."

They walked on a bit. Past the Flying Pieman. "One of my regulars," he said. "They put kangaroo meat in their pies before it became fashionable."

"It's still unfashionable," Leila said, smiling.

He liked her sense of humour. She was quick. "Oh, there's your fish & chips," he said. They were outside Papa Giovani's. Leila peeked inside. There was a curved counter displaying cakes: mini ricottas, mini cannoli, mini Eclairs ... the menu board had pizza and spaghetti marinara. "The best in Bondi," Zac said. "Although it's a bit early. Do you wanna walk on?"

"Sure."

They continued past Bates Milk Bar on the corner of Campbell and Hall. A Bondi institution. He pointed up Hall to a shop on the corner of a laneway. Ya Habibi's.

"Our competitor," Leila said.

Zac smiled. "In that case I won't tell you how many of their Buddha sticks I've eaten."

"You can tell me."

Zac laughed. "More than I can count," he said. Then added, "They have belly dancers on the weekend. Not as good as yours though."

They strolled on. They passed the Gelato Bar, another Bondi institution. "Their cherry & cheese strudels are to die for," he said. "Maybe we can come here afterwards ..."

Leila made a non-committal gesture.

"Doesn't appeal to you?"

"No, it's just ... you know, working in a restaurant every day, you start to crave home-cooked food."

Zac nodded in understanding. He thought about his father working in a butcher shop on Curlewiss Street. They had walked past it earlier—it was closed on a Sunday—but Zac didn't say anything about it to Leila. He felt embarrassed. His dad used to bring off-cuts home. Usually offal. That's what home cooking meant to him.

They came up to the Astra, now a retirement village. This was something Zac could talk about in relation to his father. "My dad's old watering hole," he said. "It was where he discovered Australians could out drink Russians!"

"Maybe he meant *some* Russians," Leila jested.

Zac liked that.

They stopped for a moment. Zac wondered if they should keep going all the way to Bondi Icebergs. The view from there across the beach was wonderful. When he suggested it, Leila agreed.

As they walked, Leila said, "You never talk about your mother. Is there something I'm missing there?"

Zac seemed to tense imperceptibly. He walked on in silence for a while. When he spoke, his voice was quieter. All the emotion was sucked out it. "She left my father when I was twelve. I haven't seen her since."

"I'm sorry I asked."

"Nah, you can ask. It's just that I haven't got much to say."

"Why did she leave?"

Zac drew in a deep breath. He let it out through his teeth, making a whistling sound. "I guess mum got sick of dad's drinking."

Leila nodded silently.

They looked back at Bondi, the golden sand, the shapely

waves as they crashed onto the shore. The beach wasn't full yet, the sun wasn't hot enough. A few brave swimmers were in the water. Surfies were still wearing full wet suits.

Later, after they bought fish and chips, they went down and sat on the grass lawn that overlooked the beach and the Pacific Ocean. Seagulls soon discovered them. Leila found them amusing. She tossed them a chip and they squabbled amongst themselves.

"Don't do that," Zac said, "otherwise we'll never see the end of them."

Leila tossed them another one.

Zac shook his head in defeat.

Leila finished her crumbed fish fillet and threw the rest of her chips at them. The noise and raucous attracted the eyes of onlookers.

Zac got up and threw his waste into a nearby bin. Leila got up and followed him, leaving the seagulls behind.

They wandered down to a different spot away from the noise.

Leila reached into her handbag and got out a book. "I brought something I wanted to show you," she said. She read off the title: "*The Prophet*. Have you read it?"

Zac looked at it. "No. But I've heard of it."

"What did you hear?"

"I'm sorry, I should have said I read a review about it. It spoke about how venerated it is. I was planning on reading it, but we just kept on getting piled up with other stuff. I suppose now I have to read it."

"It's one of my favorite books. I particular like this chapter—'Beauty.'" She opened the book and handed it to him.

He read in silence.

Leila watched him, waited for his response.

"I like this line," he said. "'Beauty is eternity gazing at itself in a mirror.' Although I'm a bit wary of anthropomorphizing the abstract."

"What do you mean?"

"Take this one for example: 'Where shall you seek beauty, and how shall you find her unless she herself be your way and your guide?' You see what I mean? He personifies beauty as some sort of being that is capable of leading us to an understanding of what beauty is. It's a tautology. And beauty is not a thing, it's not something that guides you. You guide yourself by your responses to what you experience. You see a beautiful face and you are attracted to it. It's instinctual. It's not something you have control over."

"I don't disagree, but I interpret it differently. I see him as saying that beauty has a way of beckoning you. Calling you. You don't get attracted to something unless it first has something that hooks you in."

"Yeah, that's what I'm saying. Something attracts you, but you don't know why. But I disagree about the seeking thing. We are the seekers. We seek all the time, often without knowing why we seek. We are drawn—sometimes even by ugliness—and then we turn around and there is beauty. Something very small and simple. It's totally unexpected. It's a surprise by definition."

"So you're saying ..."

"I'm saying that personifying beauty as a guide doesn't explain beauty any more than saying it just happens."

"Maybe that's what he is saying, that is just happens."

"Maybe." He flicked through some more pages. "See, here? He's doing it again. 'When love beckons you, follow him.' Really? He's saying, give in to love when he comes knocking. In reality, you can't give in to love. You can only give in to the idea of love. Love itself happens to you whether you like it or not. You can't give in to it. So his analogy is all wrong."

Leila looked confused, perhaps even a little hurt.

"What's wrong?"

"You're squashing my beautiful idea of his writing."

Zac kept a straight face, but he felt like laughing. "But beauty was your guide, surely he didn't lead you up the garden path?"

Leila punched him in the upper arm. Hard. She was serious.

"Ouch!" He rubbed his arm.

"That's for being an arsehole."

Zac smiled inwardly. He had no intention of telling her things she wanted to hear. "So you think personifying the abstract is a legitimate way of writing?" he asked, seriously.

Leila thought for a moment before answering. "How else can we get an abstract concept across otherwise?"

"Why not just show people with an example."

"I suppose. That makes sense."

"There's a concept you need to know. It's called 'The Pathetic Fallacy.' It refers to the personification of nature. It can also refer to man-made things as well, like streets and cities. For example, 'the lonely street.' As if a street can be lonely! Of course, we all know what the writer means. He means that the people living on the street don't talk to each other, they just go to work each day and scurry back into their shells. It can also mean the hero who lives on the street is lonely, he can't find his soul mate, or he has a flaw that prevents him from connecting to people."

"Yeah, so 'the lonely street' says all that in just three words."

"It does. But bad writers over-use it. And it smacks of artifice. It draws too much attention to the writing itself. Like the writer is showing off. I prefer to be more honest. Just tell it as it is."

"But then the beauty is lost. The beauty of words."

"You mean superficial beauty. Like the way you thought *The Prophet*'s words were beautiful, but they were actually quite meaningless and merely evoked an emotional reaction in you. You didn't think about what the words actually meant."

"But what if my emotional reaction is true?"

"True for you, but what's true for you may not be true in reality. Go down that path and you're well on your way to becoming a sophist."

A perplexed look came over Leila's face. In that moment Zac thought she had become a little girl again.

"What's a sophist," she said.

"A sophist," he said, "is a person who reasons with clever but false arguments. As my Literature Professor used to say: 'The intelligence used to win arguments is not the same as being true to intelligence itself.'"

After that, Leila didn't say much at all. They walked back to his car. He asked if she wanted to have a drink at the Beach Hotel, but she declined. She seemed to be lost in thought.

On the drive back to her house, she said, "I was going to show you some of my writing, but now I've changed my mind."

He said, "I didn't mean to put you off."

She said, "No, you didn't. Quite the opposite. You made me realize more than ever that I want to be a writer."

– 9 –
Point Piper

FINN walked into the lounge room but stopped short at the sofa settee. Errol Branigan Deamer was outside on the patio, staring down at the harbour like a lord surveying his domain. He must have sensed that Finn had walked into the room, but he didn't turn around.

Finn braced himself, then continued his way across the plush carpet. He quietly cleared his throat as he approached, a deliberate act to ensure he couldn't be accused of sneaking up on his father unawares.

"Ah, you're here," Errol said, turning as Finn came onto the patio.

Finn politely saluted his father with a subtle raising and lowering of his eyebrows.

"They say the weather will turn tomorrow," Errol said. "You wouldn't know it by looking at the sky."

"No."

A patchwork blanket of clouds hung over the harbor; the sun occasionally breaking through as they drifted eastward. Errol took his eyes off them and laid them on Finn. He looked remarkably fit for a top banking executive. Maybe a little paunchy around his waste, but that couldn't be helped, given the world he lived in. More than anything, he prided himself on being invisible. The man behind the money. Apart from his laundered business shirt, silk tie, and tailored trousers, the only ostentatious item he wore was a Vacheron Constantin watch, a discrete symbol of his senior position and authority. It was his lunch hour, which typically fell between 12 p.m. and 2 p.m., and usually entailed alfresco dining in Circular Quay with international business associates. But since he was here, it meant he had gone out of his way, and when Errol Deamer went out of his way, it was a clear indication that things weren't going according to his strict expectations, and that simply would not do. Not in the world of Errol Deamer.

Finn waited for him to speak.

"I've been talking to your mother. She tells me that you've changed you mind. You no longer want to do a Bachelor of Commerce. You want to do English Literature instead. Is that true?"

Finn's first reaction was one of perceived betrayal. He had expressly asked his mother to keep it a secret between them. They had talked about it, and he had told her, in the utmost confidence, that it was 'merely an idea.' All he wanted to do was try one semester, and if it didn't work out, he could always switch back. His second reaction was one of anger, because deep down, he knew that once he started he probably wouldn't turn back. 'Shoot first, ask for forgiveness later' was his plan, but now he felt like a deer caught in the headlights, frozen on the tarmac, a sixteen-wheeler bearing down on him. His third reaction was to lie—or at least mitigate the situation as best he could: "I don't want you to get the wrong impression," he said, taking the back foot. "You know what I mean? Mum has always supported my creative side. We thought—"

"—Thought what?"

"That if I did a semester, I'd get it out of my system."

"Get it out of your system? Like the time you stabbed that kid in primary school?"

Finn's face reddened. "You know that was an accident."

"Bringing a knife to school ..."

"I didn't bring it. My friend gave it to me."

Errol gruffed. "Either way, if you play with fire, you're going to get burned."

"It's only for one semester."

"One semester, one minute, I'll hear none of it."

Finn stared at his father with a mortified expression. He didn't know what to say. At eighteen, he thought that his father would treat him like an adult. He had just started on his 'L's'—it was in the intimacy of his mother's car that the conversation about his future had taken place—and so they were obviously giving him more responsibility. But this ... this was a slap in the face.

"I know what you're thinking," Errol said. "Your old man's a bastard. Well hallelujah! In my day—if I even so much as spoke out of turn, I'd get backhand across the snout—and I can tell you, my father was nothing like me. He was a hard man. So consider yourself lucky. I'm being soft on you."

Finn felt like saying, *then give me your best shot*, but he held his tongue.

Errol put a hand on Finn's shoulder. "Sit down."

Finn didn't feel like sitting, he wanted to run. Run as fast as he could and never look back. But he felt his legs weaken; he looked at the chair beside him, and took it.

Errol took the other one, sat back, and rubbed his jaw, as if remembering his father's knuckles, and looked around—at the house, the garden, the view, taking it all in, assessing it, weighing up its value, and then dropped his arm and slowly nodded to himself, satisfied that he had formulated what he wanted to say.

"I'm afraid I haven't been completely honest with you son. I know you want to blame your mother. But it's not her fault. She didn't say anything."

Finn looked at his father, unable to hold back his suspicion. Was this some sort of trick?

"Let me put it this way. It's wasn't so much what she said, but what she showed me."

"What did she show you?"

"That story of yours. The one you submitted to Varuna."

Finn felt his cheeks flush.

"She was so proud of you, and she couldn't stop talking about it. I knew then and there that something was afoot."

"She didn't say anything about English Literature?"

"Son, in my job, I have to move hundreds of millions—sometimes billions each day. To do that you have to have a sixth sense." He touched the side of his nostril for emphasis and then added: "The Japanese, you know, they call it 'reading the air.' That's who I learned it from."

"Reading the air ..."

"No one has to say anything."

Finn tried to imagine what it was like having that kind of responsibility. His first thought was: *what if you fucked up?*

"Don't look so shocked," Errol said. He enjoyed the effect he was having.

Finn momentarily averted his eyes. He felt like his father was toying with him. What did he want?

Errol's face grew serious again. "So ... anyway, it's time to get down to business. There's something you need to know. But I have to warn you. You're not going to like hearing it."

"You're going to lecture me again."

Errol considered his son's response. "Nope. This time I'm going to keep it short and sweet."

Finn didn't know whether to believe him or not.

"I want you to think about what I'm going to say now, really hard, ok?"

"Ok."

"Don't just say that—'okay,'—like you're trying to fob me off. You need to really mean it."

"How can I mean it if you haven't told me yet what you're going to say?"

"Think of it as a promissory note. If you don't repay it, the debt collector will come knocking on your door."

"You want me to make a promise?"

"A promise that you're going to fully take on board what I'm about to say."

"Why all the fanfare. Why don't you just fucking tell me?!"

"Hey! Language son. If your mother was here ..."

"Sorry. I'll use 'fricken' next time."

"She doesn't like you using any of those words. It's not becoming of a gentleman."

"Maybe I don't want to be a gentleman."

Errol snorted. "Listen son, if there's one thing in this life that's certain, you *do* want to become a gentleman. Trust me. So don't talk like that."

"Don't talk like that," Finn said, parroting his father.

Errol raised his hand in a mock gesture of slapping him.

Finn jerked back thinking he was serious.

Errol stared at him for a while, then lowered his hand. "You really thought I was going to hit you, didn't you?"

Finn didn't respond.

Errol shook his head.

A lone seagull passed in front of them, It momentarily caught their attention.

Slowly returning his gaze to his son, Errol said, "There are two great forces in life, Finn. The force to belong and the force to be free. Every single human being, rich or poor, smart or foolish, lucky or unlucky—if they don't figure out which one governs them, and if they don't do it before the age of thirty, their life won't just be wasted; it means they weren't smart enough in the first place."

"What happens if they do it *after* thirty?"

"They'll have lost ground on their competitors, although they'll still have a chance to claw back some pride—if they're lucky."

Finn took some time to process this. "So you want me to choose which one I'm governed by?"

"I'm all ears."

Finn took about as much time as he dared take before answering. It wasn't because he didn't know the answer. He knew it for sure. It was the anticipation of his father's response that held him up. His gut told him that no matter which option he chose, his father would choose the opposite. Just to piss him off. "Obviously you're expecting me to say I want to be free," he said, looking at his father square in the eye.

"Ok, and do you think that's true?"

"Yeah."

Errol sighed. "Well ... you clearly don't know yourself, do you?"

Finn felt a sharp stab of anger. And something else, a feeling that the stuffing had been knocked out of him.

Errol said, "What if I told you that *you*—Finnegan Michael Deamer—you want to belong, you just don't know it."

"How can you say that after all we've said today? When you know I want to try my hand at writing. I *want* to be a writer!"

Errol tried not to laugh. "You see what I'm saying? You want to be a writer. You don't *need* to be one. You want to be one. That's the hallmark of needing to belong."

Finn felt an inchoate pressure build up in his head. He wanted to shout at his father, literally scream at him. He clenched his fists furiously. His mouth twisted and quivered with hostility. The whites of his eyes flashed and his nostrils flared.

"Settle down son. You've still got your whole life ahead of you. It's too early to make a decision anyway."

Finn's chest heaved and he felt himself slowly regaining control.

"Sometimes I think there's some of *my* old man in you," Errol said, "the way you carry on." He gave a nod of approval. "At least you've got the passion."

"Mother says I'm nothing like your side of the family," Finn said, finding his voice again.

"Yeah, she's apt to say that. You just have to look at the photographs to see that. It's all from her side." He tapped his index finger against his temple. "But I'm talking about here. And in that regard, you're a Deamer. Make no mistake about it."

– 10 –
Randwick

JOE is convinced he killed a man. He tells everyone who means something to him that he did it. He holds his button-less flannelette shirt across his body with a disfigured hand. His shoulders are uneven and bony, and he moves with a shuffle, never stops moving, blood is agitated, and he spits a gob on the ground.

There is no body. No one can find it and no one believes him anyway. Joe can't put two sticks together if he tried, and every other word he speaks is mis-spelled.

His aunt Laura said he wouldn't hurt a fly. She told the story about Joe from a long time ago. This was to anyone who cared to listen. Joe was a musician and he met a girl called Kate. Kate lived at home with her mother and father. One day her father never came home. Sometime later she learned that he was murdered. He was found lying in a pool of blood on the concrete floor of an automobile garage.

Joe sung in a choir at the same church as Kate. One day he saw Kate's father come in and he hid behind a curtain. He heard Kate's father confess that he had molested his daughter. The priest assured the father that he wouldn't tell anyone about it, including the police.

Joe left the church and never went back. When Joe confronted the girl about the truth, she said it was over, that her father was dead.

"What do you mean dead?" Joe asked.

"They don't know who did it."

Joe couldn't sleep. He couldn't concentrate. Kate suggested he go see her psychologist. He's pretty good she said.

Joe thought about it. Several weeks past. He thought he was going crazy, so he decided to go. He told the psychologist his story. He said he murdered Kate's father and even though he felt it was the right thing to do, he felt guilty about it.

"When did you murder him?"

"About a month ago."

"Kate's father's been dead a year."

Joe didn't believe the psychologist. His memory was real. He remembered hitting Kate's father with a steel pipe. He felt the pipe make contact with the skull. He saw the big dent it made. He saw the blood.

The psychologist recommended he go see a psychiatrist. Perhaps medication would fix the problem.

They put Joe on olanzapine, because risperidone would have interfered with his music making. Joe started putting on weight. He became unhappy. He went off the medication and rekindled his belief.

To convince himself that he wasn't crazy, he went to Kate's father's grave. The gravestone was freshly chiseled, it hadn't been weathered yet. He read the inscription. It said, "Here lies John Anderson, born 4th August, 1944, died 13th July, 1992. Husband to Mary Anderson ('nee' Shaunessy) and father to Kate Anderson. In loving memory. Gone but not forgotten."

He stood there for a long time.

He put his hand in his pocket and pulled out a leather wallet. He didn't know how it got there. He opened it and looked inside. He found a driver's license. The license was in the name of Bryan Anderson, and it had a photo ID.

It was a face he would never forget.

Zac leaned back in his chair and stared at nothing in particular. For about a full minute or so he let his mind float free, a feather on the wind.

He read what he had written, then tore it out of the typewriter, balled it up and tossed into the wastepaper basket.

He started again.

Bloody feet numb from fire dancing

Hollow mouth shouting strange half truths
Worms drying out on a pale glass slide
No one's counting the forgotten dead

He trashed it.

His first thought was that the guy had crashed his bike. But as he drew closer, he noticed the man wasn't moving. When he reached him, he saw that he was lying askew, one leg draped over the frame. A Roadstar. A slightly crumpled Mercedes dealership card had slipped from his left hand. Saliva dribbled from the corner of his mouth. He looked to be in his early 60s, his hair was silvery gray and he has a bearded stubble. He looked like a wino. Adam carefully checked for signs of breathing, but the man was completely still. He glanced around to see if anyone else was there, but there was no one. It was just him and the dead man. Slowly, Adam backed away, mounted his bike, and rode off.

He trashed it.

He began writing a story about a man named Thomas Wilford. He was in a murderous mood.

– 11 –
Surry Hills

"WHY so glum?" Finn's mother Veronica—"Honi" as she was affectionately known—was staring at her son with a bemused expression, wondering why he looked so deflated when he had just graduated from university with flying colours. They were driving to Surry Hills, where she had planned a special dinner for him. Errol was interstate and couldn't make it, but he had called up earlier to pass on his congratulations.

"Your father's over the moon, you realize that?" She angled her head to watch out for traffic, then took New South Head Road.

"Yeah, I know."

"Well what's the problem then? Don't tell me this is still about your dream of becoming a writer?"

"Oh yeah, I forgot, I was supposed to grow up."

"Now you're acting like a child. It's beneath you Finn." She brushed a strand of her golden hair away from her brow. Everything about her was golden. The gold rings on her fingers, the gold earrings, the gold bracelets on her finely sculpted arms. She was wearing a chiffon evening dress threaded with gold weave. Her high heeled-shoes were mirror black with gold trim. They were on the seat beside her. Finn had to move them to the floor when he got in.

"I don't know why I have to say this. How many times have we been over this? You've got plenty of time to pursue your dreams once you establish yourself financially. And besides, you haven't fot any life experience yet. You need to live! All good writers do. You know that. Look at you! You're still a puppy."

"Mum, don't talk to me like that."

"But you are honey." She reached out to stroke his cheek but he brushed her away.

"What's wrong? You don't want to be your mamma's boy anymore?"

"Mum, I said don't talk to me like that."

"Then how to do you want me to talk to you?"

"I don't know, the way you talk to your artist friends."

Honi gave him a wistful smile. "Speaking of which, I'm going to pick up someone on the way. Is that all right with you?"

"Who?"

"His name is Kenji Ishiguro. He's a *manga* artist."

"A *manga* artist?"

"Yeah. It's going to be the next big thing."

"What's a manga artist?"

Honi looked at Finn with a cheeky sense of secrecy. "A comic artist, but not like you think. He specializes in human transformation. Human into animal. Animal into machine, that sort of thing."

"Sounds weird."

"It is. That's why I like it."

Finn looked at his mother in a new light. He had always thought she was into commercial art—hotel lobbies and corporate offices. But then again, she was being financed by his father, so she didn't have to do anything she didn't want to do. Finn didn't fail to grasp the contradiction: Here she was, telling him that he needed to grind out a boring day job while she flitted through art circles and high society, living out her dream.

———— • ————

Kenji was waiting for them at the corner of New South Head and Darlinghurst Road, under the "big Coca-Cola sign." There was nothing particularly special about him; he could have been a "salary man," one of the many faceless men who ran corporate Japan. What set him apart was his clothes. He wore a sheepskin-lined bomber jacket, skinny jeans decorated with a tassel chain, and a pair of red-skin belt buckle PU boots. Finn's first impression was that this guy had just flown into Sydney on a vintage warplane and was planning to take some R&R.

"Hi, my name is Ishiguro Kenji," he said, extending his hand to Finn after getting into the car.

Finn reached around and shook with his left hand. "I'm Finn," he said.

"Yes, I know," Kenji said, "your mum told me all about you."

"Hopefully only the bad things," Finn quipped.

Kenji smiled. "It's Japanese tradition."

Finn liked this guy already. He radiated a youthful energy that channeled an ancient wisdom that he could only guess at. "So how did you guys get to know each other," he asked, curious about how his mother came to know this guy.

"We met at the place where we're going to eat tonight," Honi said. "Kenji's friend is a sushi chef there. He's going to treat us to his culinary masterpieces."

"Do you like sushi?" Kenji asked Finn.

"I suppose it depends," Finn replied.

"Ooh, then maybe you won't like it," Kenji said.

"Don't worry, he'll like it," Honi assured the both of them.

They pulled into a narrow street in Surry Hills and parked outside a nondescript warehouse. There was a roller door and a smaller door next to it with an intercom.

Kenji pressed the buzzer and said, "*Ishiguro san-nin Sama*

desu."

After a few moments, a Japanese voice came on and said: "*Omachi shite orimashita.*"

Kenji replied: "*Arigato gozaimasu.*"

The door opened.

They climbed a set of stairs to the first floor, walked down a narrow corridor and came to another door. The words "Satsuma" was written in Japanese characters with English underneath.

Kenji knocked softly. The door opened and they were greeting by a young Japanese lady who offered to take Kenji's coat. Kenji gave it to her. She directed them to the bar.

The bar was fashioned from *matsu*, showing its sinuous grain in splendid detail. A glass display case in front of the bar was stocked with a bewildering variety of *sashimi*, almost all of which was foreign to Finn except the octopus and scallops. Above the bar were Japanese characters written out vertically, which Finn supposed was the menu. Posters showing nature scenes in Japan adorned the walls amongst other paraphernalia such as signed pictures of sumo wrestlers, pictures of famous people who had attended the establishment, and *Nihonshū* labels.

Presently a voice grabbed Finn's attention. He introduced himself as Nakamura and gave the slightest of bows. He said something in Japanese which Finn didn't understand. Kenji translated for him: "He says that he is honored for you to eat his food and he looks forward to giving you a memorable dining experience."

Honi and Finn thanked him and he smiled, then asked Kenji something again in Japanese. Kenji said, "He asks if set menu is okay, or would you like individual order?"

Honi said right away, "The set menu we had last time was wonderful, can we do that again?"

Kenji translated and 'Nakamura-San,' as Kenji called him, nodded his understanding and went to work.

For a while, Finn watched as Nakamura sliced various species of fish, and plated them up with garnishes on banana leaf. The man's hands worked fast and fluidly, each movement exhibiting the highest degree of discipline and knowledge.

Meanwhile, the female waitress brought them green tea and asked if they would like to have some alcohol beverages with their meal.

Kenji said, "*Dassai mistu kudasi.*"

"What did you order?" Finn asked.

"I chose some sake, if you don't mind. It will compliment the *sashimi* and should suit your palette."

"Ok."

The waitress returned and gave them each of them a small square bamboo cup, a *masu*, and placed an even smaller glass, an *ochyoko*, inside the square cup and then poured the sake into the glass until it overflowed and filled the square cup to the brim.

Kenji said, "I'll tell you a secret. If they give you a *tokkuri*—a small ceramic flask—and the sake is warm, it means they've given you the cheapest sake."

Finn watched intently as the waitress decanted the sake into the tiny glasses. She did it in the traditional manner, holding the bottom of the sake bottle as she did it. It was all done with an elegance and grace that Finn was unaccustomed to and it deeply impressed him.

Kenji raised his *masu* and beckoned Honi and Finn to follow suit. "*Kampai!*" he said, and they sipped from their glasses.

Finn found the sake to his liking. It was room temperature, silky smooth, and had a faint sweet alcoholic tinge to it. It was so good he took a second, bigger mouthful.

"Take it easy," Kenji warned him. "It will creep up on you!"

Finn was about to explain he can hold his liqueur when the *sashimi* arrived.

He didn't know the names of anything on his banana leaf, but he recognized a few items. One of them looked like fish roe; another he was sure were anchovies, but not in the form he was used to. "What's that?" he said, pointing to a glistening pale white specimen.

"*Ika,*" Kenji said. "Raw squid."

"Oh. I might give that a skip," he said.

"Don't be silly," Honi said, and she ate hers, saying it was divine.

Kenji ate his and concurred. He urged Finn to try his.

Finn gingerly put it in his mouth and chewed. It was surprisingly robust, popping with each bite, the flavor reminding him of the ocean, but in no way fishy at all. The *wasabi* and *shōyu* complimented it perfectly.

"Good, yeah?" Kenji said.

Finn had to agree.

"The stranger the better!" Kenji said enthusiastically, popping another morsel into his mouth.

The focus on food gradually shifted to conversation about art. Finn wanted to know more about Kenji's "taste" in art now that he knew his taste in food.

Kenji smiled graciously and answered as best he could given his limited, but surprisingly functional English. "It's very hard to explain," he began.

"That's ok," Finn said, "take your time."

Kenji called for some more tea. "If you want to know, I don't like drawing baby girls dressed in bikinis shooting laser guns, and I don't like the *yaoi* style—" seeing Finn raise his eyebrows, he said, "—how should I put it? Girls' fantasy of beautiful young homosexual men."

"Oh. Kinky stuff."

"Very kinky stuff."

Honi said, "Kenji's work is more mature. It critiques modern society at the interface of biology and machine."

"Cyborgs?" Finn said.

"No, not cyborgs," Kenji said. "It's more how spirit forces enter into machines we use and infect our bodies."

"Spirit forces entering into machines?" Finn said.

"Yeah, like in Japan we have many spirits which interfere in human affairs."

The tea came.

"So you believe in the afterlife?"

Kenji smiled. "A lot of *manga* readers do!"

"But you don't?"

"In Japan we call it *yōkai*. It means something like 'spirit world.' It usually has connection to animals or nature. The part I am exploring is how animal spirits enter into machines and awakens our hidden animal ancestry."

Honi said, "Kenji uses metaphor to reveal aspects of human nature that we have forgotten or suppressed."

"I see ..." Finn said, thinking he was beginning to grasp Kenji's thought process.

But Honi knew he wasn't even close. "I don't think Kenji is getting his ideas across clearly. What he is saying is, he draws things like the 'jellyfish man'—a man who transforms into a half-man half-jellyfish monster after getting electrocuted by his washing machine."

Kenji laughed at himself.

"Turns into a human jellyfish monster?" Finn said, incredulously.

"Yes! The electric current changed his genes. They went wild."

"That is wild," Finn said. "So what does this jellyfish man do?"

"He eats newborn babies."

Finn looked at Kenji like he was a crazy man.

Kenji smiled uninhibitedly.

"Welcome to the world of Japanese *manga*," Honi said.

They sipped some tea.

"How do you come up with these ideas?" Finn asked. He was really curious now.

"I had some hang-ups about my body when I younger, so I kinda fell into a pattern of drawing *manga* about transforming heroes ..."

Finn felt embarrassed to probe further, so he just said: "But your jellyfish man is not a hero, he's a monster!"

"No. Why? Just because he eats newborn babies doesn't mean he's a monster. He only eats babies that are infected with evil spirits."

"I see. There's a lot about your world I still don't know."

"Come and see the exhibition," Honi said. "You never come to my gallery. Maybe this is your opportunity to broaden your horizon."

"But you don't want me to become a writer!" Finn said, almost with anger.

"Honey, you've got me all wrong. I fully support you. It's just that I don't want you to suffer needlessly. Kenji here, you should ask him why he is here in Australia when *manga* is booming in Japan right now. Go on, ask."

Finn sighed, then turned to Kenji. "Ok, tell me."

"Burnout," Kenji said simply.

"Burnout?"

"Yes. I was working long hours for little pay. The competition is fierce right now, and everyone is looking for that original idea. I was getting stale."

"Your ideas are highly original."

Kenji gave a self-deprecating laugh. "Not in Japan!"

"Oh, I see."

Kenji sipped his tea again.

Honi said, "Kenji has taken up a twelve-month working holiday visa. He's hoping to get some new experiences here that he can inject into his art."

"Don't get me wrong," Kenji said, "I didn't come for the kangaroos and koala bears."

"I'm glad to hear it," Finn said.

"But I am interested in your echidna and crocodiles," he said. "We don't have anything like that in Japan."

"You can see both of those in local zoos," Finn said.

"Maybe you can take him," Honi suggested.

"Yes, I would love that," Kenji said.

"There's a reptile park up the Central Coast," Finn said. "You're sure to find what you are looking for there."

"That sounds great," Kenji said. "When can we ..."

Finn looked at his mother.

Honi said, "Why not tomorrow?"

"Sure," Finn said. "I don't have anything on tomorrow."

Honi said, "Kenji doesn't have a car, so you'll have to pick him up, like today."

"From Kings Cross?"

"Yeah." Kenji nodded.

"What time," Finn asked.

"How about we make it for lunch?"

"Okay."

After dropping Kenji off in Kings Cross, Honi said to Finn, "I didn't want to say it in front of him otherwise he would have gotten the impression that you really were a mama's boy."

"What the hell are you talking about?"

"I've set you up with an editor."

"You did what?"

Honi kept on staring ahead as she drove. She had that look on her face that said this was a mother's duty. If she had to get her hands dirty, so be it. It wasn't as if she hadn't changed his nappies a thousand times or more. As incongruous as that looked when compared to the image she projected, the golden girl of Bel Air.

"You said you want to be a writer, and so you get your wish."

"All this time you've been telling me I need to grow up."

"You do need to grow up. That's what this editor's for. She's going to whip you into shape."

"What if I don't want an editor? What if I'm not ready?"

"Honey, you know as well as I do that that's just the fear talking. But don't worry about it. I've got it all worked out. This will be our secret. Father will never know about it."

"You realize I'm starting work next week? He got me a job in customer service. Said I had to start in the basement and work my way up."

Honi looked at him. "I know. And I know how much you're going to hate it."

"You do?—you really do?"

Honi's face tightened, and she sighed with impatience. "If you only knew some of the intimate concessions I had to make with powerful men to get where I am today, you wouldn't be complaining like the spoiled brat that you are. Life doesn't hand the keys to you on a silver platter Finn. You've got to fight your way forward, no matter what it takes, if you really want it. Do you really want it?" She looked at him with a fierceness that cut through any remaining pretense.

Finn swallowed hard. "Yeah, I want it."

"You say it like you want it because your father doesn't want it."

"You know that's not true."

Honi's face softened ever so slightly. "Evelyn's going to have a field day with you."

"Evelyn?"

"Evelyn Harper. Your soon-to-be editor."

Finn stared resolutely ahead. A woman. Why did his mother think that a woman would be good for him? He would have preferred a man. Not like his father, but an artist, someone with a true passion for the art. He had always had the image of Max Perkins in his head, the guy who discovered Hemingway, Fitzgerald, Wolfe and Rawlings. So this was to be his lot?

Honi watched Finn's reaction and seemed to be enjoying herself. She turned into Wolseley Road. "I've set up a meeting for tomorrow afternoon."

"But didn't we say I was going to take Kenji to the reptile park?"

"Oh, yeah, I forgot about that. You'll have to go early so you can get back in time."

When she parked the car in the garage, she did not get out right away. Finn sensed that there was something else she wanted to say. Something important. He waited, and consciously made his muscles relax, and in that moment, he felt like he had matured a notch. He recognized that it was a really bad habit of his, to always press ahead of himself, rather than just let things happen naturally.

Honi said, "Your father married me, he said, not because he had a lousy sense of art—he in fact prides himself on his ability to distinguish great art when he sees it. It's actually part of his job. Do you know that sometimes he has to meet art evaluators for high-end customers, who've had their art stored in Swiss bank vaults and other places around the world, so that he can see that their investments are not fake?"

"You're saying he can spot a fake when he sees one?"

Honi nodded. "I'm not saying he has X-ray vision, he leaves that kind of thing to the experts, but he takes their advice, and he bases his judgment on that. The point is, he lays his eyes on work that the public rarely sees, if ever. On those occasions, he comes home, and you should see him. It's like he's had a religious experience."

"You could have fooled me."

"It's what I am saying, there's a lot of him in you. It's why I believe in you."

"You really mean that?"

"I really do."

Finn looked at his mother. Her face had softened, had a glow to it, like she herself was having a religious experience. It turned him on, he didn't know why. He suddenly thought of Evelyn, and wondered what his mother had told her, how she would receive him. He wanted to ask, but his mother had already gathered up her keys and handbag and was getting out of the car.

He got out and followed her.

He caught a glimpse of her face as she turned toward the stairs that led down to the internal entryway. The look was gone and she was all business again.

– 12 –
Central Coast Reptile Park

IT amazed Finn that Kenji could spend so much time staring at one animal. Long after Finn was bored, Kenji was still snapping away with his Nikon F90, loading film roll after film roll.

Clack-clack-clack-clack-clack-clack-clack.

He was especially fascinated with the echidna. He followed it as it waddled around its enclosure. "It's so big!" he remarked. "In my mind it was much smaller."

"How much smaller?"

"I don't know, about this much." He demonstrated with his hands.

Finn imagined him holding an egg. It didn't occur to him that he should have brought his own camera.

Earlier, a caretaker gave a short, enthusiastic talk on the animal. They were a monotreme, a warm-blooded egg-laying mammal. The baby was called a "puggle." After it hatched, the mother stuffs it in its pouch, actually just a fold of skin, and the puggle doesn't suck on a teat, but tickles a gland to release milk. They have a tongue that's about 20cm long and sticky and use it to gather up termites. Its signature look, the armour, is made of quills which they use to fend off predators by curling up into a ball. "But now I'm going to tell you something you probably don't know," the caretaker said. "The latest research suggests the ancestor of the echidna might have been aquatic. That's right. Which means that at some point in the past it diverged from the platypus family, but we're not sure how or when yet."

"I wonder how it got it quills then," Kenji said, turning to Finn.

"Beats me," Finn said.

Afterwards they made a beeline to the crocodiles. This was something that Finn could wrap his head around. A mindless, cold-blooded beast that ambushed its prey without warming. A true monster.

"So scary!" Kenji said, watching it emerge out of the water.

Here was something that Finn did know. "If you feed them chicken, they taste like chicken," he told Kenji.

"You've eaten crocodile? he said, like someone who was willing to try it had it been on a menu.

"No But that's what someone once told me."

Clack-clack-clack-clack-clack-clack-clack-clack-clack-clack-clack-clack-clack clack.

Elvis they called him, and they fed him a quarter cow. He ripped a hunk off it and threw it down his gullet. The keeper was hanging onto the other half and Elvis lunged at him. The keeper retreated and Elvis grabbed the rest and threw that down as well.

Kenji was marvelously impressed.

Finn had to admit that he just witnessed a primeval act of nature. This could have happened two hundred million years ago.

Clack-clack-clack-clack-clack-clack-clack.

On the way up to the reptile park they had talked about Kenji's life in Japan, his family background. He had come from a small family, he was an only child. "But I wasn't spoiled," he maintained. "I was brought up mostly by my grandparents, because my mother and father worked all the time."

He did have a half-sister, but he hardly knew her as they had never met. His father had her from a previous marriage.

Finn was amazed. "You've never met her?"

"No."

Finn didn't understand.

"In Japan," Kenji said, "we don't talk about such things."

"Doesn't that make you sad?"

"A little."

"Don't you wish you knew her?"

"I've seen her in photographs. I've sort of idealized her by now. I have this sepia-toned image of her in my mind. If I saw her in real life, I don't think I would be able to handle it."

"I guess you're right. It would be weird. Maybe a little too weird."

"We'd have nothing to talk about. She has lived a completely separate life from me."

"In that case," Finn said, brightening up, "maybe you would have something to talk about. You could compare notes, if you get what I mean. See how her life was different from yours."

Kenji seemed to shrink at the prospect. "I wouldn't know where to start," he confessed.

"Why—just start at the start!" Finn enthused.

"Start at the start," Kenji echoed, as if trying it out for size.

"Yeah."

"Maybe, but I don't know. We're both adults now—she's older than me. I'd feel embarrassed as her younger brother."

"I don't know," Finn said. "It's up to you."

And they left it at that.

On the way back, the conversation turned to art again. Kenji was all fired up about what he saw. He was brimming with ideas. He couldn't wait to get back to his room and start drawing. Finn felt like he had learned something: a child-like naivety goes a long way. Seeing something for the first time can leave a strong impression. If you are an artist, this can feed into your creative process. It could even lead to an obsession.

"Are you always like this?" Finn asked.

"Like what?"

"You really get into it."

Kenji thought for a moment before answering. "We Japanese—we tend to really get into whatever we do. We are very 'hands on culture.' That is why we are famous for many special art forms—making swords, pottery, creating *manga*—we have so many types. People dedicate their entire lives to just one specialty." He laughed at himself. "Yeah, so we really get into it."

"I think it's a good thing," Finn said.

"It also leads to all kinds of crazes. Like, do you remember the yo-yo?"

Finn couldn't help smiling. "I remember the yo-yo."

"People think us Japanese invented the yo-yo, because we started the craze, but actually it was around in ancient Greece. Some say it was invented by Plato."

"No way."

"Yeah."

"He was a philosopher."

"I know. But maybe he got bored one day and decided to invent a spinning toy."

Finn laughed. "Can you imagine that. Plato playing with a yo-yo."

"It's funny, I know."

"Did you ever ..."

"Play yo-yo?"

"Yeah."

"I did at school. Until it was banned because it caused too

many interruptions."

"You mean it disrupted classes."

"Someone smashed a window when the string broke."

"Ah, that would do it."

They laughed together.

"I wish my *manga* would become a craze," Kenji said, wistfully.

"Maybe they will now, because you have Elvis."

"Ah—Elvis the crocodile. He is a rock star!"

"He sure is, the way he ate that hunk of meat."

"He gets fat like Elvis too!"

"Maybe you can draw the real Elvis turning into a crocodile," Finn suggested.

"A singing crocodile."

"Yeah, he hangs out at a night club."

"And is good with the ladies."

"Oh yeah, he's good with the ladies."

They laughed again.

"You'll have to be careful though. The Australian Reptile Park could sue you for stealing their icon," Finn said.

"Ha, yeah! But only if they read my *manga*, right?"

"Yeah, it would have to be pretty popular, so famous that everyone around the world knew about it. And then they'd sue you."

"In that case, they'll never find out," Kenji said. "Because not many westerners read Japanese *manga*."

"No, I guess not," Finn said, falling into thought as he drove.

– 13 –
Ali Baba's

LEILA watched as Zac came in through the back door to the kitchen. He had been in conversation with her brother Dano in the back lane. The look on Zac's face told her immediately that this was no ordinary meeting. Dano and Zac often met out the back, where she guessed they were involved in nefarious activities. Neither spoke about it, but she guessed drugs. Normally, the routine between the two passed without fuss, and she felt that if she interfered she would only bring them bad luck, so she never spoke about it. She pretended it was none of her business.

Except something was different today, and she couldn't ignore it.

"What is it?" she asked Zac as he brushed past her to the dishwashing station.

"Nothing." He busied himself with sorting plates into a dish rack.

She pressed behind him. "Please, I know something is going on."

"I don't want to talk about it." He tried to jam a plate into a rack that was already over-packed.

Leila stopped his hand with her own.

Zac froze.

"It won't fit," she said, and took the plate out of his hand.

He gave her a frustrated look.

"Talk to me," she said.

Zac hesitated.

Leila waited.

Slowly, and with obvious anguish, Zac said, "I've got to go away."

Leila stared at him, not sure she heard correct.

"As soon as I'm done here, I've got pack and go."

"Go where?"

He shook his head. "I don't know. Somewhere very far away."

"What do you mean, 'far away'? Far away like overseas?"

"No-no! Not that far. I was thinking Darwin."

"Darwin?"

"Yeah."

"Why?"

Zac dropped his eyes. "I messed up."

"You messed up?" Leila couldn't hold back her emotions any

more. The anger came out.

Zac stiffened, as if preparing himself for a fight.

"Don't tell me Dano got you into this."

Zac shook his head.

"What did he do?"

Zac set his teeth on edge.

"What did he do?"

"He didn't do anything. It's my fault."

"Then what did you do?"

"I don't want to talk about it. Not here." The way he said it, it was like the walls have ears.

Leila tugged his arm. "Outside, come on."

They went through the kitchen and back out into Goodlet Lane where Zac had met Dano earlier. Leila looked up and down to see if Dano's car was still there.

It wasn't.

"What did my brother say to you," she demanded.

Zac tried to avoid her eyes, but she wouldn't let him. "It was a business deal," he said eventually.

"And?"

"I made a mistake."

"What did you do?"

Zac stalled.

Leila put her hands on her hips.

Zac sighed. "I may have compromised your brother."

"You did what?"

"You can't talk about this, okay?"

Leila made a mean face. Waited.

"My father's been gambling. He needed the money."

"How much money?"

"Thirty grand."

"Thirty grand?"

"Dano promised to help me out."

"How long has this been going for?"

"A few months."

"So what did you do?"

"Dano thinks I may have sold some of his product to an undercover cop."

Leila put her hands over her face. The anger she felt earlier mutated into fear.

"I know," Zac said. "I stuffed up."

She lowered her hands and looked at him. She sensed the fear in his eyes as well. "So you have to leave." She said it like she didn't believe it.

"Just for a while."

The way he said it didn't reassure her. She felt tears gather in her eyes.

Zac reached out, put a hand on her arm. "It's okay. We can write letters to each other. Yeah?"

"Letters," Leila intoned, as a tear tracked its way down her cheek.

"Yeah. It'll be beautiful."

"Love poems from exile," she said, wiping the tear away.

Zac allowed himself a smile. "You'll have to teach me how."

"Me teach you?" she said, genuinely surprised.

"Yeah. I've never written a love poem in my life."

"You haven't? Not to one other girl?"

"Never. You'll be the first."

"Does that mean we're boyfriend and girlfriend now?"

Zac searched her eyes. "Is that what you want?"

"You said our relationship was platonic," she reminded him. "If we got involved, it would spoil what we have."

"Not if I'm far away."

Leila fixed her gaze on him, her heart heavy with confusion. She felt a tangle of emotions—fear, disbelief, hope—they threatened to swamp her sense of self control. His words about their relationship being platonic echoed in her head, a shield he had always used to keep her at arm's length. But now that he was leaving, the walls between them seemed thinner, as if distance would somehow bring them closer. "Not if you're far away," she murmured.

"Yes."

"You really mean that?"

"I do."

"I'll hold you to that," she said.

"Please do," he said. His voice was gentle, like a caress.

She let the feeling flow. It helped restore her inner equilibrium. "You know, I've never seen your handwriting," she said, almost smiling.

"It's terrible."

"You'll think mine is childish."

"I've seen your writing. On the order slips. It's beautiful."

"You think so?"

"It's just my opinion."

Leila felt like saying, *you'll have to wean me off that one day.* Instead she said, "In that case don't get too used to it. I might write something messy just to throw you off."

Zac's face broke into a soft smile, but the tension between them hadn't fully dissolved. It lingered in the air like an unfinished rain shower, slowing time down. She wanted to say more—ask more—but words felt fragile, like they might shatter under the weight of what remained unsaid.

Zac said, "The messier the better. Make me work for it."

Leila was about to say something when they heard a voice come from inside. The back door swung open. It was Leila's father. At first his face expressed concern, but then it quickly turned to annoyance. "What are you guys doing? There's work to do."

"Sorry," Leila said. She scurried back inside.

Leila's father continued to stare at Zac who hadn't moved yet. "What are you waiting for? This isn't a nun's convention."

Zac let Leila's father wait that extra second then followed Leila in. As he did so, their faces briefly came within a hair's breadth of each other. Their eyes locked. An unspoken covenant passed between them. Then the moment dissolved, and Zac went back to work.

– 14 –
Pitt Street

"Okay, show me what you've got," Evelyn said. She took the sheaf of paper from Finn and leaned back in her chair, rocking it ever so slightly as she read.

Finn watched her silently, looking for the telltale clues he thought might indicate what she was thinking, whether or not she liked what she was reading.

Sam first saw it from the corner of his eye. A luminous streak across the gloom of the night sky, as if a razorblade had slashed open a dark curtain revealing a fiery glow from within. That can't be right, he thought. Nothing flew in his world. Nothing except the smallest of bugs. And this wasn't a bug. He was sure of it.

He scanned the sky again. The apparition was gone. But something deep in his gut told him to run. He was half a block away from Jim Bob's house, a rickety, old cobbled-together shack of flotsam and jetsam. Instinct took over. He bolted forward, legs pumping hard, like a rabbit darting for its hole.

He burst into Jim Bob's kitchen, breathless, words tumbling from his mouth in a rush of syllables.

"Hold steady young man. What are you babbling on about?"

Sam pointed to the sky. "There! I saw it!"

"What did you see?"

Sam faltered. The image in his mind still fresh, but words refused to form. "It was, it was ..."

Jim Bob wasn't like the other adults who inhabited this soot-smudged, acid-eaten town. His left hand was a mangled mess, three of his fingers were whittled down to gnarled stumps. One of his eyes lolled in his head, the echo of a brutal wound. Most folks kept their distance from him. In fact, they kept their distance from all children. They never had a kind word for them. They gazed down upon them with cold, hard eyes, treated them worse than stray dogs. Many of the kids were reduced to starving waifs. But Jim Bob was different. He never talked down to Sam. He was always there for him. Listened to his questions with genuine patience, no matter how crazy they sounded.

"Slow down and tell me what you saw."

"It ... it flew!"

"It flew?"

"Yes!"

Jim Bob's gnarled hand search for a chair. He pulled it up and shakily sat down. His good eye flicked back and forth in disbelief.

"What? What is it?" Sam asked.

"That thing you saw…" he said, with a trembling voice, "they cut it out of our mouths, like ripping out our tongues. Only the forsaken know what they're called. And we wished to God we never heard it."

Sam felt an icy chill creep through his veins.

Outside, the streetlights flickered like dying fireflies. They cast an intermittent glow into the room through its one grimy window. It made the shadows in the corners writhe and twist, almost as if they were alive. Far off, Sam heard a metal garbage lid clatter to the ground. Probably a mutt. He hoped it *was* a mutt. Then nothing. Just the sound of their own ragged breathing.

"What are they called?" Sam dared ask.

"Screechers," Jim Bob intoned, the word hanging in the air like a death sentence. He shook his head. "They were supposed to be gone. Driven to extinction during the last great surge. I don't understand …"

"So what now?" Sam asked.

Jim Bob shuddered. "All I can tell you is if their bellies start churning, you'd better skedaddle indoors. 'Cause if you don't …" He trailed off. His right hand unconsciously rubbing the stumps of his left hand.

Sam looked on. A horrible revelation came to him. Maybe now he finally understood why.

Jim Bob turned towards the window. His one good eye, staring, unblinking.

Slowly, as if drawn by an invisible force, Sam shuffled to the window and squinted through the grime.

The night outside seemed darker, the shadows deeper—hungrier. "So they're back," he said, unable to believe the truth of it, even as he said it. And almost right on cue, as if they had been listening to his innermost, deepest secrets, a distant, bone-chilling shriek split the night air.

Evelyn sighed, put the papers down on her desk. For a long time she didn't say anything.

Finn fidgeted nervously while he waited.

"How should I put this?" she began. "It's good. The atmosphere is thick with tension. The characters are okay. The setup has potential. But what's the story here? Where is this going?"

"I'm not sure yet. It's just an idea I had."

Evelyn shut her eyes. Rubbed them, then opened them again. Refocussed. "Don't get me wrong. I know what you're trying to do. You're obviously trying to emulate Stephen King."

Finn just stared at her.

Evelyn cracked a pat smile. "Come on, it's not that bad!"

Finn turned his gaze away, to the windows, to the day outside.

Evelyn said, "Listen. You can obviously string words together.

So why don't you write something closer to home. Something local. You know what I mean?"

Finn looked at her again, tried to gauge her seriousness. "I've been reworking that story about the doppelganger," he said. "I think I figured out why they cloned him."

Evelyn was shaking her head.

"What?"

"It's B-grade. Anything with clones will always be B-grade."

What have I got to do here? Finn thought.

A silence fell between them.

Evelyn tapped a cigarette out of a pack that was lying on her desk, lit it, then drew back hard and blew out a long stream of smoke. "We've been at this, for what, two weeks now? We still haven't passed first base."

"I've been writing every day. Scribbling like a maniac."

"Maybe that's the problem. You're too close to the trees. You're missing the forest."

"What forest?"

Evelyn gave him a self-deprecating laugh. "I'm getting too old for this. I really am."

Finn tried not to take the bait. He was only too aware that his mum had set this up. Who had ever heard of an editor giving up her precious time to coach a wanna-be writer? It just wasn't done. Yet here he was. He just hoped there wasn't any money involved. That would have really been the death knell for it.

"The thing is ... there's something you need to know." She took another puff of her cigarette. Tapped some ash into her ash tray. "A writer needs to come from a place of moral outrage. You hear what I'm saying?" She eyed him carefully. "What pisses you off?"

Finn considered her question, nodded his head. He had heard this before, but not quite as succinct as this. Zac had said something similar. He couldn't quite remember the words exactly. Of course, there was a whole bunch of things that pissed him off. His job. His office manager. His mum's refusal to let him move out of home—because he was her "little boy." He knew she was joking of course; he lived in Point Piper. Why would anyone want to live anywhere else? His inability to get a roll on in his writing. This last one really pissed him off. But none of these things could be sustained for a whole novel. A short story maybe. A vignette. But that wasn't what Evelyn was asking, was it? "What pisses me off," he said, realizing the one thing that did piss him off.

"I was going to say your father, but somehow I don't think that would be a smart choice—for a number of reasons," Evelyn said, tapping the ash off her cigarette.

"No, it wouldn't."

"But at the same time, we need to find the fire. I'm not feeling it. Are you?"

"You mean, do I think I'm a writer?"

Evelyn swatted her hand through a pall of smoke. "Let's not get ahead of ourselves, shall we? We're just trying to solve one problem at a time here. We need a story. That's all. Do you know what a story is?"

"Do I know what a story is?" Finn asked, as if he was being treated like a kindergarten kid.

"Yes," Evelyn said, leaning forward. She stared at him intensely.

The way she looked at him, it unnerved him. She was actually putting him on the spot. Zac would have loved that!

Evelyn waited patiently.

"I can tell you what a friend of mine once said." He made a big effort to pull himself together.

Evelyn raised her eyebrows expectantly.

"He said ... a story teller is like one of those old bards in ancient times. You know? Around a camp fire, they tell a story. If they're good, they get something to eat. If they're bad—well, they probably get eaten. I mean, they probably get stoned to death first." He smirked, thinking Evelyn would appreciate his response.

Evelyn kept a straight face. She wasn't impressed.

"You don't agree?"

"Oh, I agree," Evelyn said. "I agree wholeheartedly. I was just thinking about the gun I've got under my desk."

Finn looked at her aghast.

Evelyn held her expression for as long as she could then burst into laughter.

Finn felt a flood of relief. He couldn't believe he took her so seriously.

Evelyn said, "So this writer friend of yours ... he sounds interesting."

Finn agreed. "He is. He majored in English Literature. He's taught me a lot about writing."

Evelyn almost choked on herself. "He did?"

"Sorry, I mean, yeah—he tried to teach me."

"Does he still teach you?"

"Ahh, no, he's gone up north. He's decided to pack it in and work on the trawlers."

"Trawlers?"

"Yeah, fishing trawlers."

"Yeah, I know what trawlers are. I was just thinking, that's an odd thing to do. I suppose ..."

Finn shrugged, like he didn't want to talk about it.

"What sort of stuff does he write about?" Evelyn asked.

"All sorts of stuff."

"For example?"

Finn thought about the many stories that he and Zac had talked about. There was the one about the son who ran a pre-fab concreting business—in debt up to his eyeballs. Loaned the money from shady financiers. When he couldn't pay the interest back, they broke his hand with a baseball bat. Next time they were coming for a lot more. His father meanwhile was dying in a hospice. On his last legs. His two sisters were coming down from interstate on a mercy run. It was going to be the last big family gathering. The mother had warned them not to talk about money ... and then there was the one about the cloned secret agent who deliberately put his clone in the line of fire to draw out the enemy. He had to laugh at that, considering what Evelyn had said about clones.

"What are you smiling at?" Evelyn asked.

"Oh, nothing."

"So are you gonna to tell me what he writes about?"

"Yeah, oh yeah. There's this one story I think you'll like ..."

– 15 –
Point Piper

DETECTIVES Phelps and Mooney walked stiffly into the lounge room where they remained standing until Honi Deamer invited them to sit.

"My husband will be with you shortly. He's just coming out of the shower. While you're waiting, would you care for some coffee?"

"Coffee will be fine thank-you," Phelps said.

Mooney nodded in agreement.

Honi went off into the kitchen while the two detectives patiently waited in silence. They both looked around the room, at the Brett Whiteley, the expensive lamps, the mini-marble sculptures, the family photos on a mantelpiece, the glorious view out across the harbour. It was that in-between hour—late afternoon fading into early evening—the sun had swelled into a blood-orange fireball, while the upper sky remained bright, rendering the water a vivid steel blue.

Honi came back carrying two coffees on a tray with some biscuits. Kingstons.

Momentarily, Errol Deamer entered the room, barefoot. His hair was still partially wet and combed back, revealing a thinning scalp. He wore a pair of linen trousers and a casual open-necked shirt.

"You have to excuse me," he said. "We just had a swim. Nothing like a dip to invigorate the old bones. We're still suffering from jet lag."

"Long flight from London," Phelps said.

"Twenty-seven hours with a stop-over in Singapore."

"Tiring."

"Business class takes the edge off, but it doesn't cure jet lag. I think I can feel the morning coming on."

"I guess we timed it perfectly then," Phelps said. "It's the end of our day."

"You want a beer instead then?" Deamer asked.

Mooney's eyes lit up. "It's tempting ..."

Deamer waited.

Phelps said, "Nah, maybe afterwards."

Deamer sat himself down in a recliner opposite the sofa, where the two detectives sat like schoolboys. Despite the relaxed air of his appearance, his face was a mask of worry. Honi came over and sat on the arm of the chair beside him and draped her hand over his shoulder. "I suppose this is where we say we're ready to hear whatever you've got to say," Deamer said, putting on a brave face.

Phelps straightened his shoulders, took in a big breath in, then let it out again. "We've got good news, and we've got bad news," he said. Seeing Deamer stiffen, he said, "But it's not what you think."

Deamer slightly elevated his chin, but said nothing.

"As you know, Finn's been missing for three, getting on four days now. When we don't hear word of someone for that long, it usually doesn't bode well. But we're not giving up."

"No."

"We're currently running leads, but it's still early. So anything we say will be pure speculation."

"Speculation is my middle name. Let's hear it."

The two detectives looked at each other. It was decided Phelps would do the talking. "First, the good news. We're no longer investigating your son for the murder of Zacharia Levin. The reason being ... our search for Finn has taken precedence. Without him, our investigation can't move forward."

"That's the good news?"

"That's as good as it gets."

Deamer leaned forward and clasped his hands together. "I thought I made myself clear when you first called us in London: our son had nothing to do with Zac's death."

"I understand. We heard you. But we have to go on whatever information we uncover, and at this stage, Finn cannot be ruled out."

"So you're saying you've got other suspects?"

"We do, but Finn is at the top of the list."

Deamer was shaking his head. "No, this won't do. You're obviously not doing your job properly. Finn would never get involved in something like ... what you're talking about. He was brought up to respect others. He's an extremely intelligent lad, and—" he searched for the word. Honi finished it for him. "—and quite sensitive."

Phelps did his best to disguise his opinion. "I understand. It's always difficult in situations like this, for the family particularly. Those who are close. It can sometimes cloud their judgment."

Deamer practically jumped out of his chair. The only thing that stopped him was Honi's arm clamping down firmly on his shoulder. "Let me explain something to you, detective—"

"—Phelps."

"Detective Phelps. In my business, objectivity separates the men from the boys. It's why I'm in the position that I'm in. I make decisions for very powerful and wealthy people, and they trust me precisely because I'm objective. Now, this comment of yours, that I'm 'family.' Why don't you just come right out and say it. I'm his father for Christ's sake! And you think that makes me all mushy inside? Then you've got me wrong."

"Then perhaps you can straighten us out," Phelps said coolly. "Tell us why you think your son wasn't involved in this business. When he was the last person to be seen with Zac, who we know is dead—the scuffle most likely took place on Lady Martin Beach, and we know Finn changed his clothes mid-way through the party—"

"Party? What party?"" Honi asked, cutting in.

"Right," Phelps said, taking a deep breath. "Finn held a party to celebrate the success of his book—"

"—Here?" Honi said, pointing to the floor as if in disbelief.

"Apparently, yes," Phelps replied in a calm voice. "And it was during the party that Finn's girlfriend noted that—"

"—Woah, hold on!" Honi said. "This is all a bit sudden. You have to excuse us, we're still jet-lagged. Did you say Finn's girl-friend?"

"Yes," Phelps replied. He deferred to Mooney.

Mooney consulted a small notepad and said, "Miss Sorbonne. Nikki Sorbonne."

"That's sounds French," Honi said. "I was not aware that Finn had a French girl-friend."

"I see," Phelps said. "Well, she is indeed French. She works as a model for Ralph Lauren. She came out here on a shoot, said she met Finn that day after she arrived."

"Where did she say they met?" Deamer asked, apparently un-phased by this new information.

"At a book reading," Phelps said. He turned to Mooney, who said, "Dymocks, in George Street."

Phelps took note of the differing responses between husband and wife and said, "As I was saying, it was Miss Sorbonne who noted that Finn changed his clothes halfway through the party, something that a model would be observant of—I think you'd agree—and when she asked him about it, he kind of just fobbed her off."

"What has this got to do with Zac's murder?" Deamer asked pointedly.

"Ah!" Phelps said. "Bear with me for a moment. You see, earlier, Miss Sorbonne saw Zac leaving the party in pursuit of his girl-friend—it was over an argument of some sort, we're not exactly sure what it was about—and she saw Finn run out after Zac. And then she saw Finn later on again, in a new change of clothes, but she never saw Zac again."

"So all you have is circumstantial evidence," Deamer said.

Phelps looked at Mooney for a moment, then nodded.

"In that case, I don't know what you're talking about," Deamer said gruffly. "It's all hearsay to me. I thought you gentlemen would be into facts, not quibbles."

Phelps said, "Unfortunately, in this case it's all we have to go on."

"What I want to know," Deamer said, "is where is my son? What information have you got on him?"

Phelps cast his eyes downward, his face betraying an uncomfortable doubt. Slowly raising his eyes again, he said, "As we explained, our investigation has stalled, but we're not giving up. What we do know is he took his wallet with him, but in the whole time he's been gone, he hasn't touched any of his bank accounts. Which of course is a serious concern."

"I see," Deamer said gravely.

"Yes, and what little information Miss Sorbonne could give us, hasn't produced any leads. We've spoken to Zac's girl-friend. She hasn't been much of a help either."

"At least that explains the missing bottle of Port," Deamer said, off-handedly.

"Missing bottle of Port?" Phelps inquired.

"Yes. A 1950 Colheita."

"What is the significance of that?" Phelps asked.

"Besides being worth a pretty penny, the fact that there was a party here, that explains its disappearance."

"I see," Phelps said.

"Don't take my word for it," Deamer said. "Here, I'll show you myself." He directed them down the stairs to the lower level, where, standing next to the laundry was a solid wooden rack full of boutique wines.

"Here," Deamer said, pointing to a vacant slot. "It should have been here."

"Right," Phelps said. He and Mooney perused the other bottles. "Nice collection," Mooney said.

Suddenly, in the quiet and confined space of the corridor, Deamer turned to Phelps and Mooney and said, "I just want you to find my son." He was visibly crumbling.

Phelps looked at Honi, whose expression—which had been a mixture of confusion and pain up until now—transitioned to one of shame.

Phelps pretended not to notice and suggested that they return to the lounge.

The four of them shuffled back up the stairs, the two detectives casting long glances at Finn's bedroom door as they passed, whereupon Phelps said, "We should mention that we interviewed Miss Sorbonne here the other day, and she showed us Finn's room. Do you mind if we have another quick look to refresh our memories?"

Honi and Deamer stopped, it took them a moment to process what was just said to them. Deamer didn't care, he waved his hand at them to do whatever they wanted. Honi nodded and ushered her husband up towards the lounge, then let the two detectives enter the room.

Despite having splendid views across Sydney Harbour—over a low-lying hedge—and having it own en-suite bathroom, the detectives were more interested in examining the floor and what was on Finn's desk. Finn's typewriter was still there, with a half-typed page still in the spool. Phelps wound it through so he could read it again, as a point of interest, finding the same description of a Japanese man eating at an *izakaya*. The description was unfinished, it left off mid-sentence describing the man chewing some freshly grilled fish.

Mooney found the carpet clean, no signs of blood stains or

broken glass—he was thinking of the Colheita. The book shelf, with Finn's surfing trophies caught his eye. He admired them, asking about Finn's exploits. Honi said Finn spent a lot of time in the water when he was younger. His interest gradually petered out, however, when he became interested in writing.

Phelps went through some other papers on Finn's desk. All of them seemed to be related to writing. "Perhaps it would be good if you can leave everything as it is," he said, satisfied with what he saw, "in case we need to come back and do some more forensics. It doesn't seem like anything untoward happened in this room. But just in case."

Mooney was of like mind. If what ever happened to Finn was sinister, it happened somewhere else in his estimation.

Honi asked what he implied by that.

Mooney said, "We can't rule out the possibility that your son was kidnapped."

"Kidnapped?" Honi said, almost shrieking.

"It's just one of several working theories," he said, trying to keep her calm.

"Oh dear," Honi said. She became teary and started shaking her head.

"I'm sorry," Mooney said. "I didn't mean to upset you."

Honi stood like that for a while, wringing her hands, trying to make sense of it all.

"I think we've seen all we need to see here," Phelps said, coming up to Honi and Mooney, putting a gentle hand on her shoulder.

The act seemed to snap Honi back to a semblance of control. She said, "Please don't tell my husband."

Phelps and Mooney gave her a long hard look, then Phelps said, "Let's return to the lounge, shall we?"

Back in the lounge, Phelps said, somewhat absently to Deamer, "Oh yeah, I forgot to mention ... we sent the local police out to your Byron Bay holiday house to see if there was any evidence that Finn might have gone there. We got the key from the neighbor as instructed. Unfortunately, we found no evidence that the house had been visited by anyone since you said you were last there."

Deamer and Honi took this in.

Mooney looked at Phelps, his look suggesting that perhaps they end the day there.

There was a general feeling that the detectives would leave, but Deamer seemed to have worked himself up into a state and said, "All of this is Zac's fault. You realize that?" He specifically addressed both the detectives and his wife.

"How so?" Phelps inquired, curious at the sudden turn of events.

"He was the one that put all those stupid ideas into my son's head. To become a writer and all of that."

"Honey dear," Honi said, laying a hand on her husband's. "I think the detectives don't need to hear that."

"No, please, indulge us," Phelps said.

Honi glowered at the men, that it had to come to this.

"He was a shitty influence," Deamer said.

Honi began to protest, but Deamer shut her down with a cutting gesture. Directly to her, he said, "All of this wouldn't have happened if it wasn't for Zac's influence. I could see it with my own eyes. How could you not see it?"

Hearing this, Honi at first displayed shock, but it was almost instantly replaced with anger. "Is that what this has come down to? You're blaming me?"

"You encouraged him."

"As a good and decent mother should!"

Deamer slapped his forehead. "I'm not against my son dreaming of becoming a writer, but—"

"—He is a writer!" Honi exploded. "He just published a successful novel!"

"A successful novel!" Deamer retorted. "It's nothing but adolescent nonsense."

"Is that what you think? Is that what you really think?"

"It is."

"That's not what I heard you say to him when sales started soaring. You remember what you said? 'Great job old boy!'"

"Yes, and then I said, 'But don't let it get to your head.' Remember that?"

"How could I forget? You've never once given him a compliment without following it up with a backhand in the same breath."

"That's a father's job!"

Honi slumped herself down in the nearest chair in frustration.

The detectives watched all this with practiced calm.

"If I may ..." Phelps said.

"What!" Deamer snapped.

"We did speak to his publisher ..."

The Deamers stared at Phelps as if they hadn't heard right.

"She told us that Finn originally got his idea from Zac."

If the Deamers knew about this, they feigned ignorance.

Continuing, Phelps said, "When asked if that amounted to copyright infringement, she assured us: 'Ideas are as cheap as chips.'"

"What's your point?" Deamer inquired.

"My point is ... even if ideas are cheap, Zac may not have seen it that way."

"It's a bit late to worry about that now, don't you think?" Deamer said off-handedly.

"I supposed it is," Phelps said, "but we can also look at it as another angle on what caused all of this."

Deamer was rapidly losing patience. "What caused all of this is Zac filling my son's head with sawdust. I don't give two hoots about whose idea it is. All I care about is my son is missing and you're standing here talking about writer's feelings. "You should be out there, don't you think"—he pointed to the harbour through the patio windows—"searching for him."

"You're absolutely right Mr. Deamer," Mooney said, tugging at Phelps' sleeve.

Phelps lingered for a few moments more, studying Deamer with a calculated calm, wondering what role he played in all of this, not just over the last few weeks or months, but bringing Finn up from childhood. What kind of ideas did he put into the young boy's head?

– 16 –
Point Piper
Eight months ealier

FINN stared at his typewriter. The whiskey sour on his desk bubbled gently, the dew running down the side leaving concentric damp marks on the loose stationary he had scribbled some notes on—notes that he had taken during sessions with Evelyn Harper. They had started out as half-hearted attempts to please her but gradually morphed into life lessons that made him feel smaller and smaller, his goal more distant with each passing day. It was as if she had undergone a vow to completely dismantle then rebuild him in her image.

The editor living through her protégé.

Did he have what it took to please her, to prove that he was more than a hack?

On more than one occasion she had told him that if he was a

bad writer, there was nothing she could do for him. There was nothing that anyone could do for him. But if he was a good writer, there was hope; she could turn him into a better writer. Not great. Not a genius. That sort only came along once or twice in a century. A freak of nature. And Finn, by her estimation, was far too normal to qualify.

Normal ...

He hated the word. Or to put it more bluntly, he hated himself for hating it. It was proof that he wasn't a lightning rod. A diviner placed on earth to capture the magic sent down by the gods.

The first thing Evelyn did was send him to an old friend of hers. Catelina. A never-married, school teacher who taught English and who had missed the boat. Childless and horny as a goat.

It was from Catelina that he learned what it really meant to be passionate about writing. She fucked him like the world was coming to an end and read poetry to him while they lay like sunning otters in the afterglow.

Her passion was infectious, and even though he was convinced he would never be a poet, she turned him on to words like they were droplets of ambrosia.

Empyrean, azure, succulent, dragoon, marmalize, impale, sagacious, undulate, pungent, votive, honey.

Honey?

Yeah she said. Nectar of the gods.

Honey and yogurt. Honey drizzled over walnuts. Honey and

milk. Leatherwood. Smoke and chipotle.

Honey and soy chicken wings he responded.

They went out and bought a kilo and cooked them up with cayenne pepper.

She caught him looking at young girls.

You like that? she asked.

Evelyn said I've got to start thinking like a serial killer.

That's dark, she said. Why don't you write about something beautiful. Like young lovers during the Enlightenment.

You mean young lovers who are part of the Enlightenment, like inventors, writers, explorers?

Yeah, explorers of the human spirit.

I'm already committed to the story.

She doesn't know you like I do.

I think Evelyn thinks I'm a business proposition.

She can do that. She's got a heart made of quartz.

How did you two meet?

We were lovers once.

Oh.

Have you ever written anything.

No, but I've inspired many a student. They're my canvas. My Great White Whale.

Have you ever fallen in love with one of your students?

All the time. It tears me apart.

Am I your student?

No.

Collaborator?

No.

Muse?

She liked that.

In that case, how about this one ... 'People: Eat, Fuck, Die'

You mean the Nihilist's Survival Bible?

Yeah.

It's been done before.

All the more reason, he thought, that he should stick to his original idea.

Evelyn said, why don't you just start with a list of all the girls? Name each one and tell their story. Since you started out with Whinnie, work backwards, one by one until you get to the first.

He read something about the first one being the most intense. If the word 'sacred' could be applied to any of them, then she would be the one.

He felt dirty.

The filth of human behavior was boundless in its depravity. Why couldn't he just write about something wholesome and clean, like Catelina suggested?

Are you chickening out on me? she asked.

No. Yes.

Sort of.

Put your ego aside, she said, and just write. Don't get attached to it. Just state the facts. Humans need a mirror held up to themselves. They pretend to be nice and caring, but at the end of the day if they were stuck in a life raft out at sea and were starving to the point of going crazy, they'd eat their own babies, mark my words.

Wouldn't you get the odd person who'd refuse to do that?

What for? So they can be a dead hero? Dead heroes don't get to live through painful memories. They don't have any stories to tell.

They make monuments out of them.

Yeah! So other people can tell lies about them.

He felt like banging his head on the table. This was getting him nowhere. He was stalling.

It was time to get real. See what he was made of.

That's my boy! she exalted.

If you want to make an omelet, you're gonna have to crack some eggs.

That gave him an idea. He'd start by thinking of each victim as a hatchling. He took a carton of eggs out of the fridge and poked a tiny hole in the top and bottom of exactly seven of them, blew out the insides, made an omelet—Ha! Without cracking a single one—then with a magic marker, he labeled them: Lisa, Billy, Francis, Amina, Sandra, Peggy, Whinnie.

One, two, three, four, five, six, seven.

If he was going to do this, he was going to have to start thinking just like—

In the words of Jim Morrison, his brain needed to be squirming like a toad ...

Lisa was vivacious. A classic redhead. Freckled upturned nose, cute as a button, a wholesome body tight in her bell-bottomed jeans. She used to twirl her purse by its strap as she sashayed up and down the strip, beckoning customers with that hypnotic sway of her hips. What fine legs! Who couldn't resist a piece of arse like that?

Thomas Wilford of course.

But being his first, well, he wasn't going to talk about it. She was part of him now. That's all he was going to say.

Finn figured it had something to do with the way it went down. The victim struggled, nearly got away. Or she begged for her life. Not just begged, but told her story in a way that got under his skin. You see ... he wanted them to be objects. He didn't want to see them as human beings. They were an image in his mind. He was an artist and they had to conform just right to what his fantasy dictated. It wasn't personal. He treated them just like any artist treated a model. Lay like that. Raise your left leg a little. Lower you arm. Tilt your head. Put your right hand on your thigh. Click-whir.

He didn't like them talking too much. Just light banter would do, thank-you very much. He didn't want to know what their dreams and aspirations were. He didn't want to know if they had any kids. That was a showstopper right there. The minute one of them said they needed to get home and tuck that little one in, it was over. He'd toss them out, just like the fisherman tosses the small ones back into the ocean.

Then he'd get real mad. God help the next one he caught.

That's what happened to Billy ...

Billy, Billy Billy.

What will we do with you?

Billy was a tomboy who she swore like a truck driver. Her thick, dark hair was cut short, with a fringe. She was one of the first to adopt a nose ring. Her eyes were big as black pools, but a sense of fear oozed from them, despite her tough outer image. She was a whole lot more feminine once he got her clothes off. Her milk white breasts were on the large side, pendulant, and hung over a soft round belly and chubby hips. Wilford had to ask why her legs were all knocked up with cuts and scrapes. Pig farming she said. Chasing the little fuckers around the yard. Arse-over-tit in the mud, that kind of thing.

What were you doing chasing them? he asked.

Where do you think you get your bacon from? she said.

He broke his rule. Now he was real mad.

He hog-tied her, ran a noose around her neck, then pulled on it until she quit struggling.

Afterwards, he fucked her in every hole, then took a bunch of Polaroids.

He put her in the water the same way he did Lisa, tied a few lengths of chain around her waist, slashed her belly open, then threw her overboard at the mouth of Balmoral Bay, right where the current took them out past the heads.

Francine.

Oh boy, Francine.

She like to call herself Frank, "Let's be Frank, shall we?" and then she'd pout with that little mouth of hers. The way she sucked her thumb was enough to drive anyone wild, male or female. She didn't like to talk about her life and Wilford loved that. She talked about the other girls on the beat instead. She knew each one by name and loved each one like a sister. She was the one that, when she went missing, got the cops into over-drive.

Wilford had to lay low for a few months after that. He'd sneak out at night, after his wife had fallen to sleep to masturbate to his Polaroids in the garage.

Where were you honey? she'd ask as he crept back into bed.

Oh, just looking over some drawings. I had some ideas I couldn't put to rest.

It was around this time that Wilford started keeping a journal—if it could be called that. He purchased some primary school exercise books with ruled lines and began compulsively writing out his fantasies. These were crude, rude, and brutal. Wilford never meant them for anyone's eyes other than his own. He wrote without censor, and without conscience. In a revealing passage, he talked about a painful period in his life, the time when he transitioned from primary school to high school. Up until the end of primary school, he felt he fit in, he felt like he was in control and was on top of things. But something happened when he went to high school. It was like he hit a brick wall. All his peers moved on, they matured. He felt like he was frozen, stuck in time. The things that interested his peers in primary school no longer interested them in high school. He didn't understand it. It was like everyone was speaking a different language all of a sudden, like he was an alien living amongst humans.

It was during that period when he started to turn inward. He found his own fantasy more reassuring than the reality of the world outside. It was also around this time that he got the first inkling that something wasn't quite right with his mind. It happened to him one day when he found a porn magazine in a neighbor's trash. The images shocked him. It opened up a whole new world that he hadn't even conceived of, even though he knew his parents must have gotten up to something to produce his two sisters and brother.

Half-sisters and brother that is, because the truth was, he didn't know who his biological father was. His mother took him away before he was too old to remember. It was something of an elephant in the room between them, because she steadfastly refused to reveal who the father was. As he grew older, the question gnawed at him. What angered him the most was his mother's secrecy. If he even so much as even hinted that he was going to ask, she totally clammed up. The man who gave birth to your sisters and brothers is your father she told him.

He refused to accept it. It fostered a rebellious streak in him. And after he hit that wall going into high school, he spent most of his time in the library, reading. He read whatever he could get his hands on. He felt that the more he learned the more independent he would become. Because that was his answer to his mother's embargo. If she wasn't going to tell him the truth, then he would fashion his own. The library also offered him something else: medical books. He studied them avidly. Especially the surgical manuals. He got off on the gore. It excited him. By the time he became a young adult, he had become addicted to slasher movies and consumed as much porn as he could, masturbating sometimes as much as eight time a day.

He wasn't stupid. He knew he was conditioning himself. By the time he got his first girlfriend, a docile lass he met at the University of Sydney during his first year studying architecture, he was no longer interested in ordinary sex. She dropped him the moment he asked her if she would like to be tied up while making love.

He worked part-time as a tradies' laborer, saved enough money to visit his first prostitutes. These girls, he found, were more amenable to doing certain things for that extra tip. He choked a couple of them to near death, and got a thrill out of it.

And then everything changed. He met Margaret, a very intelligent arts student, who swept him off his feet. He decided to reform himself. He threw all his porn away, he stopped seeing prostitutes. He put all his energy into his career.

But deep down inside, the beast continued baying for blood. It took a heroic effort of will to suppress it. Twice, he failed. One time when he felt a girl up at a crowded railway station. She cried out and he ran. He decided to be more prepared next time. He cold-jumped a university student walking home one night after she had gone out with some friends to the Coopers Hotel in Newtown. He had watched her, saw how drunk she was, and followed her as she tottered fearlessly down the back streets, first down Hordern, then along Mechanic and lastly turning right into Church. He ran up behind her and punched her in the side of the face knocking her to the ground. He got his arm around her throat and dragged her into St Stephens Anglican church grave-yard, where, much to his delight, he got to do his thing amongst the tombstones. He pulled her shirt up and bit her breasts like a rabid dog, then raped her vaginally. She couldn't scream because he stuffed a sock in her mouth and bound her hands with cable ties. When he was finished he left her there sobbing under one of the many trees that shaded the cemetery, his identity safely concealed by the stockinged mask that he wore.

He promised himself he wouldn't do it again, but reading the papers over the following days excited him so much he knew he was going to make a liar of himself. And this is how, after all the years of building up to it, he came to realize that he was sick, desperately sick, and how—writing in that scrunched up childish lettering of his—he came to call his affliction, "My Secret Disease."

– 17 –
Circular Quay—Manly

Finn saw Kenji first, he was scanning faces in the crowd and had not yet noticed him as he stood waiting at the entrance of Wharf 3, wearing faded jeans, a short-sleeved open plaid shirt, a white T-shirt, neon-green Nike Airs, and a pair of cat-eye sunglasses.

When Finn waved, Kenji finally noticed him and walked over. "I didn't recognize you with those sunglasses on," he said.

Finn took them off and smiled. "I use them to hide the bags under my eyes."

"Jeez, you look wasted man."

"I've been off work."

"You're not feeling well?"

"Nah, I feel great. I'm just having long nights on the piss."

"Writing huh?"

"Nose to the grindstone."

Kenji looked over to the ferry information board. "So you want to go to Manly today?"

"Yeah, why not?"

"Sure, why not."

The ferry ploughed through a stiff breeze, Finn's shirt flapping hard against his body as the two of them stood in the prow enjoying the rise and fall of the hull against the waves. Finn thinking the whole time about the way bodies might or might not get dragged by the currents after being dumped in the harbour. He figured out that Wilford had cut their bellies open on the foredeck, then rolled them over the gunwale. There would be some blood. He'd wash it off with some sea water drawn up with a bucket on a rope. The only catch was driving his boat to the entrance of Balmoral Bay. It was a pain in the arse, because he had no one to help him when he got back to his mooring buoy. Normally, someone would be standing at the bow, gaff hook ready to scoop up the buoy and tie the line off. Doing it alone meant he had to time it just right, then run to the front, while leaving the boat unhelmed.

It was for this reason that he always made sure to pick the calmest of nights to do his thing.

It made him smile inwardly. He wondered if the cops would ever figure out the pattern.

If anyone asked why he turned around after rounding Gubbah Gubbah, he could always say that he was having engine trouble. He'd dump the body exactly when the boat was facing due south, from the port side. The only person that might see anything, was if they were standing somewhere along North Head, and that was highly unlikely at 3 a.m. in the morning.

Kenji expressed delight when the ferry rolled heavily as it crossed the heads, the long frequency waves coming in hard from the ocean.

Then it calmed down again, and they motored towards Manly jetty.

They walked over to Manly beach, threading their way through a river of tourists. They each grabbed a kebab along the way, Kenji opting for chicken and Finn for lamb.

They sat down on the northern breakwall, dangling their legs as they ate, and watched the beachgoers who covered the golden sands like confetti.

"It's wild," Kenji said between mouthfuls.

"Yeah," Finn said, absent-mindedly. He was gazing on a group of young women who had just arrived. He watched them wriggle out of their clothes. One of them was wearing cut-off jeans and had a great body. He thought that, maybe she is self-conscious, or maybe she isn't, but the way she was undressing, he could have imagined she was doing it in the privacy of her bedroom. And then as soon as he had that thought he berated himself: *Fucking hell, what am I thinking?* He was one step away from planning a rape. He shook his head, as if trying to rid himself of some cobwebs that had stuck to his face.

"What's up?" Kenji asked.

"It's just a fly," he said, opting to lie.

Kenji said, "The flies are really bad here I noticed, compared to Japan."

"You have to keep your mouth shut in summer, otherwise you'll end up having an unplanned meal."

Kenji pulled a disgusted face.

"Aerogard," Finn said.

"Aerogard?"

"Insect repellent."

"Oh, that stuff. I think I know it. It smells of bad aftershave, right?"

"Yeah, it's unpleasant, but it sort of works."

They chewed for a bit.

Finn said, "And sunscreen. If you go out into the sun and don't want your skin to turn to leather, you need to wear it."

"All right."

"Aerogard, sunscreen and thongs."

"Thongs?"

"See what everyone's wearing on their feet? They're called thongs."

"Oh, b-san we call them."

"B-san."

"Yeah."

Finn quietly laughed.

The sun was fairly high in the sky, the clouds were thin and spread out, the wind was slightly on the strong side, but that couldn't be helped; all in all it was a glorious day. Finn took his shirt off and put it on the ground next to him.

Kenji was wearing a designer jacket made of Japanese denim. He followed Finn's example and took it off and folded it neatly and laid it by his side. He had a white T-shirt on underneath with the words 'Your love warm is happy' in newspaper font lettering. There was a cute creature underneath that looked like a cross between a jelly bean and a teddy bear bearing razor sharp teeth and sporting a wicked grin.

Finn felt he could take that several ways. "Does that have any meaning in Japan?" he asked.

"This? Nah! It's just cheap clothing from a dollar shop."

"I didn't know you were a cheapskate," Finn said jokingly.

"Cheapskate?"

Finn had to think about that one. "A person who cuts corners as much as he can when spending money." He mimed cutting the corners off a square as he said it.

Kenji got it. "Oh, yeah, I see. I do! I cut every dollar. I have to. *Manga* artists like me don't make very much. I have to ask my parents for money to survive."

"Really? That bad?"

"Yes. That bad. Actually, when I said I came here to get new ideas, that was ... I guess I should say, a little bit untrue."

"How so?"

"It's kinda hard to explain."

"Try."

"You haven't heard of it, I'm sure. It's called Otaku. How can I explain ... *eh taw neh*. I suppose the best way to describe is to say 'a person who locks themselves up in a room all day and only watches video and *manga*.' Usually very weird stuff. Also, they just do low pay jobs. Like convenience store. And they never talk to anyone."

"Sounds like social anxiety to me."

"Yeah, maybe a little bit of that too. But basically, they want to be cut off from society."

"Isn't that a very un-Japanese thing to do?"

"It is! But what I wanted to explain, is that just recently, we had a big case in Japan."

"Oh yeah?"

"Yeah, there was this weird guy, and he killed some little girls and they found his room full of *manga* and other stuff. And so they said he was *Otaku*, and so *manga* is now associated with this bad person. Especially people like him who read weird *manga*, like raping and killing young girls."

"Holy shit, they do that there? Allow *manga* with those kinds of things?"

"Unfortunately, yes, they do."

Finn was shaking his head. "So you came here to escape the heat."

"A little bit, yes."

"But you don't draw *manga* like that, do you? No. You said you did—what do you call it?"

Kenji said, "Transforming humans into—" he almost said 'weird' but then checked himself—"into strange things. But not rape and murder of little girls."

"I'm relieved to hear that. Except, I have a confession to make."

"Yeah? What is that?"

"I'm writing a story about a man who rapes and murders young women."

"Oh."

"Yeah. It's pretty heavy."

"In that case, I should tell you about Miyazaki."

"Miyazaki ..."

"The guy who did those bad things. But I'm not going to say it was *manga* that made him do it. He was already crazy—in my opinion."

Finn nodded. "So what did he do?"

"It's very weird shit man. I tell you. He was a ... how should I say? A deformed person?"

"Like he had a deformity?"

"Yes. His hands were deformed. It caused him to be bullied in school."

"That can do it."

"And he lived like *Otaku* in his parent's home. But his parents were always working, never home. So his grandfather was his companion. But then his grandfather died. And so Miyazaki be-came even more lonely. Watching all those videos and *manga* day and night, and his mind must have become, you know, we say, *Baka*. Crazy."

"Yeah, right, but we're not going to say *manga* caused him to go crazy, right?"

"No. He was already sick, to do those things."

"And so what happened then?"

"This is where it gets bad ... he took a little girl and strangled her to death, then had sex with her body. Afterwards, he took some of her bones and teeth, crushed them to powder, and sent them to her parents with a note saying something like, 'Here is your daughter.'"

"Jesus."

"Yeah. He did this to other girls, and even ate them, you know, like an animal."

"So he was a cannibal."

"Yes. That's it. A cannibal."

"And then what happened?"

They caught him, I think when he tried to take another girl. There were two sisters, he separated them, one of them ran off and called their father."

"Boy-oh-boy. So how many of these did he do?"

"Four I think."

"Ok."

"And now he is in prison and they will, you know, hang him,

I'm sure."

"For sure."

They reflected individually for a while, finishing their lunch. Finn, for his part, felt a little agitated by what he had heard. His agitation stemmed from two sources. The first was that some of the things Kenji had said disturbed him. It made him realize that he had not fully thought through just what kind of individual Wilford was. What truly motivated him. The second was that his conception of Wilford, compared to this Japanese killer, seemed tame by comparison. Perhaps, in failing to fully flesh out his motivations, he had overlooked some behaviors that Wilford probably engaged in? Thinking this, he turned to Kenji and said, "So what do you think motivated this guy, you know, to do the things that he did?"

Kenji wiped his mouth with a paper serviette and, thinking for a moment, said, "You're asking me if I know what goes on in the mind of someone like Miyazaki?"

Finn looked at Kenji honestly and said, "I supposed I am, yeah."

Kenji looked out at the ocean, his eyes fixing on the horizon. "Actually, there was a big debate in Japan about who Miyazaki was. On one side, the media portrayed him as a pervert—I think you call it. They said his interest in 'cute girl' *manga* was proof that he refused to grow up, that he had a 'two-dimensional complex.'"

"A two-dimensional complex?"

"Yeah, that's what they called it. It's like *manga* drawings are two-dimensional, right?" He laughed sarcastically.

Finn kept on looking at him, absorbed by what he was hearing.

Kenji said, "But you know, there was this one guy, a *manga* artist who was also a writer and critic, he actually came out with an article in support of Miyazaki. Yeah! Can you believe that?"

Finn's eyes widened.

Kenji nodded in the affirmative. "I didn't know him personally, but we all talked about him. It was very important to us, as *manga* artists."

"What did he say?"

"He said something like ... he and Miyazaki were pathetic figures because they both liked to hug dolls. It was something in their hearts, they went to pieces—I'm not sure how you say it— fall apart?"

"He fell apart hugging a doll?"

"Emotionally."

"Oh, right, lonely, yeah."

"But get this. He said the only difference between him and Miyazaki was that Miyazaki needed to hug them too much, you know? He made the mistake of putting too much force into it, he said, and killed them."

"He said that?"

"Yeah, something like that."

"Jeez."

"He admitted he was an extremely shameful figure, but we have to imagine Miyazaki hugging his doll and falling to pieces. It's—how do you say?—a terrible image, but we have to imagine it if we can."

Finn tried to imagine it. He saw this pathetic, weakling of a man, hugging a human-sized doll and crying, rocking back and forth, hugging harder and harder until—but no ... something didn't make sense. It couldn't have happened that way. Strangulation was a violent act, he knew that much from his research on Wilford. The victim usually struggled. A lot of force had to be put into it, at least for several minutes. There was nothing pitiful about it. It was vicious and brutal.

"We were all deeply affected by it," Kenji admitted. "For a while I felt ashamed. I stopped drawing. I kept on thinking that there were men out there that would look at the pictures I drew and think about things I couldn't control."

"But isn't that the nature of art?" Finn responded. "Once it gets out there, we have no control over it."

"For sure. We agree that art doesn't cause people to do bad things. But the connection is still there, don't you think? Like, I don't know, synchronized somehow."

Finn straightened up. "What does it mean, synchronized?" he asked, somewhat perplexed.

"Good question. It's funny, when I think about it," Kenji said. "I remember seeing a picture of Miyazaki's bedroom, with its thousands of videos and *manga*. What surprised me is that it doesn't look that much different from my own room."

"In Japan?"

"Tokyo."

"Right. So by extension, that makes you—"

"—*Otaku.*"

"Yeah."

"I know." A sad expression crossed Kenji's face. "It's why I came here, to get away from it. To clear my head."

Finn let Kenji brood on his emotions and didn't say anything for a while. There was something in Kenji's words that made him feel queasy. Like here was a person that was directly affected by the kinds of ideas that he was writing about. And they weren't even his ideas! What was he getting himself into? He wondered if Zac had actually thought his idea through, that he was throwing a hook out there and hadn't considered what he might dredge up. Or had he? It made him start to think about what kind of guy Zac really was. How well did he really know him? How well can you know anyone?

Kenji broke Finn's thoughts, perhaps talking more to himself than to Finn directly. "This Miyazaki business has made me question for the first time—what is the difference between someone like him, and me? If I was honest, I have to admit that I have many strange things in my mind. Some of these I draw, others fade away. The ones that keep coming back ... they're the ones I draw. In my imagination, anything can happen. That is true. Except ... it's all two-dimensional. Not real. You can't find what I draw in real life."

"So what are you saying?"

"I think what I am saying is, we all have monsters inside us. The only difference between someone like Miyazaki and me is I keep it in here." He pointed to his head.

– 18 –
Waterloo

LEILA's heart rejoiced with a flutter of beats when she saw the letter from Zac on the kitchen table. Picking it up, she noticed right away that others had examined it, the evidence of their sweaty finger prints along its seam. She held it to her chest and ran up to her room.

After closing the door behind her, she lay stomach down on her bed and using her finger, gently pried the letter open. Inside were several pages of writing on blue-lined paper. It began with a poem:

I will not speak of hearts enfolded by doves' wings
I will not dream of lips' tender caress
The moon does not sing luminous love songs

For lovers longing happiness

There is no reason for rain to touch our skin
Or gift us tears we never kept
'Cause time has whispered its dying promise
While souls lingered where shadows slept

"I do not wish to make you sad," he wrote. "There is something eternal in sorrow, which kindles a light more brightly than fleeting joy. For the depths of love we ought to plumb if we are to be honest writers." He then went on and described his circumstances in Darwin, living in a share house with "three no-hopers," who "ran their days out like a dripping faucet."

But Leila wasn't absorbing the words anymore. Zac's poem had vexed her and all she could think of was wild, thrashing seas that crashed on craggy rocks in huge plumes. She wanted to grab his hair and pull it out. She paced around the room like a caged animal. Words of hatred flew from her lips. "The bastard! The dirty, lying bastard! Pathetic fallacy! What does he think he is doing? Does he think I am his plaything?"

She tore the letter up. Once, then twice. Then she cried. Long and hard. After the sobs died down, she collected the pieces, wet with her tears, and slowly pieced them back together again. She had to creep into her father's makeshift office which also served as a telephone room, where he kept an assortment of consumables, like pencils, erasers, paper, gluesticks and sticky-tape, and there, very carefully, she stuck the letter back together again.

"What are you doing?" inquired her younger sister Maria.

"It's none of your business," Leila snapped, and she ran back to her room.

Her heart had caught fire and nothing in the world could extinguish it except ice cold words.

She opened her most recent journal and began writing:

I feel like you wrote your poem with the precision of a surgeon, knowing exactly how much pain to inflict. It's been an unspoken promise between us, that I am your slave and you are my master. On more than on one occasion you have raised angry red welts across my ego, but this time, you have drawn more—you have drawn blood. It's like you want us to become tragic figures, like Heloise and Abelard.

I can feel the push-pull working on me now. One part of me wants to interpret your poem as a declaration of 'love by its absence.' It's a canny technique, sure to pull in a sucker like me. But since we have known each other for almost a year now, another part of me is telling me to block my ears to your siren call, and sail resolutely by.

The problem is, it may already be too late. I can feel your spell starting to work its alchemy. It is affecting the very words I am writing now. I would say ... it is almost like your hand is hovering over mine, guiding it against my will.

I have to fight it with all my might.

And yet, more than once I swear an incubus has visited me at night. Except I can never make out his face. I am always too terrified and swoon uncontrollably. I unconditionally blame this on your sworn injunction against us having sex, that it would spoil the beauty of what our minds have forged.

And the whole time you've had the decency to avoid asking me if I'm a virgin!

I am not going to use the "rape" word, that would ruin what we have created, but it sure as hell feels like it in terms of what you have done to my mind.

And just before you think these words are too strong, look at what you have written: <u>For lovers longing happiness</u>.

When you said you would send me "love poems from exile" I expected to get something dry, authentic, like polished bones. But then you broke your own rule—you anthropomorphized! Yes! I <u>know</u> you did it deliberately. What I don't know is why? I have wracked my brain and the only answer, the best answer I can come up with is you want to show me that the master is fallible. That he is human. Is this your way of trying to make me fall out of love with you?

If it is, it's not working. Come home now. I don't want to wait any more. I am made of flesh and blood, not metaphors.

My dad knows about us, I told him. He hasn't made his mind up about you yet. I suspect he is happy that you are far away. He likes to think that his daughter is pure and clean!

If you don't come back ... I don't know what I will do. All I can say is it won't be a cliche. I won't throw myself off a bridge as would be expected of a mad Lebanese woman. I suppose I can thank you for that. You have planted the seed of belief in my mind, and it is growing. I know that now. It's just that this is a very critical time for me. One wrong weather pattern, a flood or a drought, and it could spell the end.

I say this because I have been thinking a lot since you have gone. It is like your absence has awoken something in me. We've discussed how my father expects me to follow in his footsteps. He had his hopes set on Dano, but he has all but written him off. Ever since he kicked him out of the house last year. So that just leaves me and Maria. Maria as you know is in year 12, but what I haven't told you is she has already told mum and dad she wants to be a teacher. So that leaves just me. Because it's also a tradition in our culture for the eldest daughter to be obedient and sacrifice herself.

But I don't want to. I want to be a writer. I want to travel the world and experience things, and write beautiful stories.

I feel like, if you don't come back soon, my dream might die. I need you to remind me of its importance.

Please come back soon!

Love, Leila.

After signing her name, she put her pen down, exhausted. She had poured herself out, saying things she would never say directly to his face. It was true, it felt like his hand had guided her, yet she didn't regret it. She just wished she had added that if he really wasn't going to come home soon, if that's what fate had decided for her, then she would go out, get drunk, and get laid. Do all the things she had fantasized about while the night was unveiled.

She would break his spell.

Even if that meant ripping her heart out.

– 19 –
Dymocks
George Street, Wynyard

Finn tried not to fawn over Nikki Sorbonne. He carefully tucked away his sense of entitlement. His luck with women. The ease with which they fell into his arms. This one, however, was different. She didn't come specifically to see him. To hear him. It was a coincidence. She had walked in off the street, curious, to see what all the fuss was about.

Finn reading from his debut novel My Secret Disease.

The crowd was fairly large and there was a buzz in the air, the kind that can be felt when there is a "happening" taking place. Finn was nervous, and said so in his opening: "I'm going to read from my book now ..."

The audience was filled with all sorts, from young to old. There was a fair share of yuppish-looking, smart-dressed young women in the front row, their sense of self wrapped up in the knowledge that they were in the company of other creatives whose destiny was not a matter of if, but when. Some even had a pedigree of their own. Short stories published in magazines. Self-published pamphlets of poetry. Jobs as junior editors. It was, just as Evelyn had predicted, a "literary affair."

But then Nikki walked in and stood at the back. The George Street Dymocks bookstore now full to the bleachers. Most of her body was concealed by those standing in front of her, but that didn't detract from her presence. It was the poise with which she carried herself, the way she held her head—slightly tilted as if she were appreciating a melody—that reminded him of a Dionysian muse. She gazed at him coolly and he found himself assenting her presence with a subtle eye flash, and a faint smile.

Slowly, he returned his gaze to the book open in his hands. Only to discover he had flipped to a completely different page than the one he had intended. Nevertheless, his eye caught the words, 'It makes me laugh how misinformed the public is about who serial killers really are ... and the police for that matter.'

These were the words Finn put into Wilford's mouth. He got them by scouring numerous serial killer confessions, psychiatrist's reports, police reports, and most important of all, forensic evidence obtained from crime scenes. What impressed him most about all this material is that it was nothing like what he had seen on TV or in the movies.

Finn had noticed that in TV, serial killers are depicted as diabolical masterminds satisfied with not just killing, but taunting police. They deliberately leave a breadcrumb trail of evidence so that it becomes a game of cat-and-mouse controlled by the killer until the ultimate scene, where the hero detective flips the script and solves the case. In police reports, they are often depicted as ogres, hunchbacks, and drooling monsters with predatory expressions. They are vile, ugly, and can be spotted a thousand yards away.

What Finn found was something rather more prosaic. Serial killers are mostly ordinary looking men, sometimes even handsome, and they use their guile and lack of fear to slip into people's lives with flattery and chivalry, or at other times, by ninja attack, stealth-style. By the time the victim finds out the truth, it's too late.

But that was just the superficialities. As Finn dug deeper, he ran into another myth: namely, that serial killers were created by bad socialization. Thinking about it, however, it didn't make sense. Not socially, not scientifically. Serial killers were actually extremely rare. It was true, many children grow up in dysfunctional households and suffer deprivations and self-esteem destroying punishments, often with mostly absent fathers who terrorize the family when they come home to take what they want. If the socialization theory was true, there ought to be a deluge of serial killers out in society, but it simply wasn't the case.

Finn had no choice but to conclude that serial killers were born, not bred. Socialization played only a small role, usually only in the first years after birth and depended on genetic vulnerabilities. For example, if there was a significant delay between the time the child was born and when it first clung to its mother's breast, it might later develop an unconscious sense of abandonment. This wouldn't be obvious in any sort of conscious way. The individual might only feel a vague sense that human connections eluded them. Or they might feel it as an inchoate psychic hunger, leading them stalk other human beings for comfort.

The social theory of serial killers, Finn discovered, came about as a result of a misunderstanding over what a psychopath and a sociopath was. A sociopath was indeed the kind of individual who was socially constructed. They had violent fathers, or mothers, or both, were probably sexually abused as children, were abandoned, tortured, had learning difficulties, and as a consequence of all these insults became hardened to the world—and themselves, and ended up acting out against the world, usually violently and hatefully. Their behavior was public, aimed at lashing out at a society that had mistreated them. Many ended up in prisons. Some reformed, when they learned that the insults they received were caused by ignorant and bad people and could be overcome with learning and self-respect.

The psychopath was a completely different animal. They were born with a genetic flaw that caused them to become psychologically "stunted." Their brains failed to mature past the pre-teen stage. Even though their bodies matured into the outward appearance of adulthood, their brains retained many of the behaviors held over from childhood: cunning, poor impulse control, a strong drive for self-gratification, and the ability to flexibly imitate—this last trait enabled them to give the appearance of maturity, easily deceiving people who themselves based their lives on superficial appearances. But above all, the psychopath was secretive. Their behavior was never public. They lurked in the shadows, and their secrets stayed in the shadows even after the harsh light of reality had been cast upon them. They were pathological liars, a trait that enabled them to hide the painful truth of their shameful acts.

Which was another myth about psychopaths—that they didn't feel pain. They felt pain all right. Except they could only feel it for themselves. As for their victims, they felt nothing. They were nothing more than objects to fulfill their monstrous need for self-gratification.

Summing up these thoughts, Finn briefly scanned his audience, then plunged in:

It makes me laugh how misinformed the public is about who serial killers really are—and the police, for that matter. They have this image of the hunter and hunted, where the hunter constantly taunts the police until he is caught. He is clever and diabolical, and driven by some twisted fantasy. He is narcissistic to the point of megalomania.

What they don't realize is that he is just the average person. He is no different from the guy next door. He has desires, hopes, he wants to make something of himself. He wants to be useful to society. The problem is, deep down he is rotten. Rotten to the core. I wish to God I was never born sometimes. Why did He make me so weak? I have tried to fight this, but the force is just too strong. A man can only take so much!

And when it comes over me, it's like a tidal wave, carrying me forward and down, down, down, and I start regressing, and the real person inside me—the one I keep buried—begins to surface. It's like I become hypnotically obsessed. Everything becomes heightened, and the merest hint of the erotic—a scantily clad woman in a bikini, a lingerie ad, pictures of cheerleaders in magazines—sets my mind ablaze, like a grass fire sweeping through me. It leaves me smoldering and brooding, an itch that just has to be scratched.

How does it start you ask? It's hard to say. Usually it's an argument with my wife. I can never make her happy. I am never good enough for her. If it happens to coincide with a bad client, that makes it all the worse. It's always this or that revision to a perfectly good design. And always at the 11th hour, after I've put all the paperwork in. It just makes me feel so drained. I lose all motivation. I end up on the couch and I waste hours procrastinating. You'd think it's depression. But it's not. Nor is it boredom. It's hard to describe. If anything, I'd call it ... incubation.

And what is being incubated, you might ask? Malevolence. That's what it is. A desire to tear the world apart. To possess it. And my targets? The women of the world who truly incubate something of value: a new life. They don't have to work for it like I do. All they do is surrender to biology's demands. Well, so do I …

It's like a crack in the dam that slowly propagates then suddenly the whole wall collapses and I break into this new realm. That's when I have to go out and start looking. I'm looking for something to let my frustration out on. Usually, I already have an idea. She was there all along. I catalogued her in my mind from a previous encounter. She's got something I want. It could be the way her mouth goes a little crooked when she smiles. Or the shape of her body. Or the colour of her hair.

The next part is the best part. The anticipation. The planning. You might be surprised to hear that the act is a little bit of a downer compared to all the planning, but it is. It's hard to describe. The world's never perfect. It never is.

And after it's all over, after I'm sated by the kill, the force recedes. The monstrous fixations, the excitability—they fade into a flat, featureless memory, which I toss into the basement of my mind with all the other junk that's been piled up there, gathering dust.

You're wondering if I feel guilty about what I've done? My answer is simple. It's not me. I didn't do it. It's the other guy. The one who can't keep his hands out of his pants, is constantly perusing porn and masturbating while high on dope.

Let me tell you, having this disease is no fun. It eats you alive. Every time I take a victim, another part of my mind has to be sequestered—locked away from the light of day. It's eating me up. I know that. But what choice do I have? All I can do is live with it and hope that one day I'll put it all behind me. Just writing about it, right now, I already feel better. It helps me put some distance between myself and the disease. But only for a while. Soon, the force will return. I know it only too well to doubt it. And when that happens, no one is safe …

The whole time Finn read this, he kept his head and eyes down. It was like a part of him was living it; he knew it, but it couldn't be helped. He felt like Evelyn had gotten a voodoo doll and was sticking pins in it, and he was the victim. She was the one who had set this in motion, suggesting he take some sick leave and go down the rabbit hole. Sick! Ha! He was sick. And the medicine? The whiskey sours he was knocking back, alone in his room, with the curtains drawn while the Doors played repetitively in the background. She had magically ignited a voice in him that he thought wasn't possible, not with his limited life experience. What was that she said? Yeah: "If you must know, Finn, some people are young in body, but old in soul."

If only Zac could see him now. He wouldn't recognize the person he had become.

Dare he say he had become a writer?

– 20 –
Light Brigade Hotel
Woollahra

AFTERWARDS, after question time and the obligatory book signings, Nikki came up and said that she was intrigued by what he read. It sounded "philosophical," she said, and it surprised her, coming from someone who looked so young and to be honest, someone who looked more like a "surfer than a writer."

Finn said he needed a stiff drink to calm his nerves. Would she care to "come with" and put up with some more of his "philosophical musings"?

"Sure. Where do you want to go?"

"I have a favorite watering hole," he said.

He drove her in his mother's car. He explained that his parents were on a river cruise down the Danube. They wouldn't be back for a couple of weeks.

He took her to the Light Brigade Hotel in Woollahra. It was fairly quiet pub with comfortable seating and draft beers. Finn wasn't sure what to order. She accepted a house wine. He got himself a schooner of VB, the old workhorse. The whiskey sours could wait for later.

Nikki told him about her modeling contract. She was doing a folio for Ralph Lauren. It was nothing special. She was the "B" model in case the "A" model got sick, or production fired her. It meant she had to turn up every day and go through the motions, but none of her photos would ever make it into the final cut. Not unless a miracle occurred.

Finn said he never thought much of miracles until he met Evelyn. He told her about the way she had turned him into a "writer." Her tricks and mysterious ways.

Nikki laughed. She asked if he regretted it. Considering the subject matter he had to deal with.

Finn told her the truth. The idea for the novel wasn't his. He gave himself one concession though. He said he didn't steal it so much as "appropriate" it.

"Appropriate it," Nikki said, laughing into her glass. "That sounds so philosophical."

"Maybe I'm a philosopher after all," Finn responded.

"In Europe," Nikki said, "people steal each other's work all the time. It's a cut-throat business. But we've got it down to a fine art. We say it's not the theft that counts, but the way you rearrange it to make it look original. Did you rearrange it to make it look original?"

Finn thought a while before answering. He couldn't help thinking he was looking at the most beautiful women he had ever laid eyes on. But now that he was sitting in front of her, he started to notice things, like her hands weren't exactly the most beautiful he'd seen before, the fingers were a little short and maybe the proportion of the hand to the arm wasn't quite right. And even though she had the most attractive face, he realized there was a recognizable asymmetry to it—he couldn't quite put his finger on it, but it was like one half of her face was slightly squashed compared to the other.

Still, he felt himself falling, and he meant falling without a parachute.

"I'm not sure I can say I rearranged it," he said at length. "But I had to flesh the whole thing out. All I had was a vignette to start with."

"I'm not sure that qualifies as theft then," Nikki decided. "Maybe you stole the concept. But what's a concept?"

"You're asking me what a concept is?"

"Yeah, I mean, I could tell you my definition, but I want to hear yours first."

Finn smiled. He liked this girl. She was already getting down to the meat. "You want to know what I think a concept is ..."

"Yeah."

"I suppose it's an idea. Like the kernel of an idea."

"That's your definition?"

"I wouldn't call it a definition."

Nikki laughed. "And here I was thinking you were a philosopher."

Finn laughed at himself, relieved that he no longer had to live up to that image. He said, "When I think of a concept, I think of compressing an idea down to its essence. Like a serial killer who murders women is killed by one of the women he intends to murder."

"That's your book."

"Yeah, if you want to describe it that way." He thought about what he had said, and added, "But it's not a very sexy way of describing the book if marketing is your goal."

"Marketing is everything unfortunately."

"Not unless word of mouth takes over."

"That's also a kind of marketing, though, when you think about it."

"I suppose you're right."

"But all the marketing in the world won't help you if the original idea stinks. If it's propaganda rather than art."

"What do you mean by that?"

"What I mean is, artists who are motivated by a socialist agenda. They get funding because they agree to do something to help a social cause dictated by politicians or activists. It's done under—how should I say?—the promise of education."

"Right. Whereas ..."

"Whereas real artists don't give a fuck about what the public wants or needs. They just live for one purpose, and one purpose only, and that is to honor their muse."

"Ah—ever the muse."

"Yes, the muse is all important. Without it, great art would never exist."

"I'll drink to that," Finn said. He downed the dregs of his beer. "You want another one?"

"Sure."

A short while later, Finn returned with the drinks and stopped—he literally froze. Zac was standing at the table where Nikki sat, his back turned, so he didn't react immediately. But then Finn saw Nikki's expression, her face tight, her eyes flicking between Zac and himself. That's when Zac noticed, and he turned. He looked at Finn with a gaze that was unmistakably filled with stone-cold bitterness.

Nikki thought Zac was going to walk up to Finn and punch him in the face. His right fist was clenched. His elbow cocked.

Finn was standing there like a lost child. His mouth quivering, trying to form words that refused to come out.

It took Nikki to get up and say to Zac, "I'm not sure what this is about, but Finn and I are sharing this table."

The spell that had gripped Finn dissolved, and he sauntered over and joined Nikki, put the drinks down and said to Zac, "Mate! What a surprise!"

Before Zac could say anything, Finn said to Nikki, "This is Zac Levin. *The* Zac Levin."

Without any artificiality or hesitation, Nikki enthusiastically stuck her hand out. "I'm Nikki Sorbonne," she said. "Finn has told me so much about you!"

Zac seemed to imperceptibly relax. He slowly raised his hand and shook hers. "In situations like this it's normal to say, 'I hope it's all good,' but somehow I don't think that'll be necessary ..."

"For sure," Nikki said, and she invited him to take a seat.

Zac pulled up a chair and sat down. His appearance was strikingly different from the other two. Finn was self-consciously dressed like a freshly-minted author: he wore the obligatory black T-shirt under a shiny gray suit, perfectly creased, with polished maroon patent leather shoes and a matching black belt and silver buckle. His hair had been freshly cut that day, and he was cleanly shaven. Nikki wore stone-washed designer jeans that accentuated her perfect legs, duck egg blue platform loafers, and a casual gauze shirt that revealed a lace black bra—which covered, rather than supported, her youthful breasts.

Zac by comparison was ragged. His jeans were marked by heavy grease stains, which were practically worn through in the seat of his pants and knees, and white jogging shoes that were scuffed, cracked, and dirty from over-use. He wore a limp green flannelette shirt over a faded blue T-shirt that looked like it hadn't been washed in months, and he carried a faint odor of woodsmoke about him, as if he had spent the night camping by a fire. His hair was still its usual short length, black and curly, like steel-of-wool, and he had a full beard—which explained why Finn didn't immediately recognize him (or didn't want to recognize him) when he first laid eyes on him.

Finn said, "Let me get you a drink." And before Zac had a chance to respond, he walked off to the bar.

Nikki said, "We were just talking about your contribution to Finn's book." She smiled sympathetically.

"Finn's book," Zac said, unable to help himself.

"Tell me, where did you get the idea from?" Nikki said. She held him with her eyes, long enough to make him feel like she was completely his.

Zac said, "That's a long story ..."

"I'd love to hear it."

Zac quietly laughed. "You wanna hear my version and compare it to Finn's is that it? You two ... going out together?"

If the question caught Nikki by surprise, she didn't show it. "No. We just met."

"What, here?"

Nikki smiled. "No. I happened to stumble into his book reading. I just arrived from Paris yesterday. My brain is still fuzzy."

"So that's your excuse."

"I'll take whatever I can get right now." She flicked a strand of hair away from her face.

Zac didn't mind her answer. Maybe even liked it. He certainly liked her look. The way she seemed comfortable with herself.

"So what did Finn tell you? That *My Secret Disease* was a throw-away idea, that it didn't matter if he stole it?"

Nikki thought for a moment before answering. "He said you only gave him a 'kernel' of an idea. He still had to weave it into a complete story."

"Is that what he said?"

"Yeah—you don't believe me?"

"No. I believe you."

Nikki waited.

"It's ..." Zac stalled, he needed to think this one out. "It's true I only gave him a skeleton of an idea ... but it was one heck of an archaeological find!" He couldn't help laughing at his own commentary. "You know? I mean, I gave him more than just a skeleton; I gave him the meat, the sinew, the nerves."

Nikki allowed herself the slightest hint of a cheeky smile. "So you basically gave him a dead body. Which means he still had to bring it to life."

Zac couldn't help chuckling at her wit. It gave him time to come up with an equally witty reply. "Yeah, so it looks like we have a full-blown Frankenstein on our hands, doesn't it?"

They laughed together.

Finn came back with the drinks. He put them on the table. "What are you guys laughing at?"

Nikki said, "Oh, we were just joking about your book."

Finn visibly tensed.

Zac passed Nikki a look to say, Right on!

Finn said, "So what's your assessment?" He addressed both of them.

Nikki looked at Zac—Zac back at Nikki. Still looking at her, he said, "I'm speaking for myself ... I read your book on the way down." He indicated his backpack which he had placed on the floor beside him. "I couldn't believe it man, you ripped me off."

"Now wait on—"

—No you wait!" Zac said turning on Finn. "You never asked me permission if you could use my idea, did you?"

Finn's face, normally golden and suntanned, turned a bright red. "How could I? You never gave me a forwarding address, not even a phone number. You never even wrote!"

Finn's words momentarily threw Zac off balance, but he quickly regained himself. "In that case, you shouldn't have written it in the first place!"

Finn stared at Zac in disbelief. The guy had clearly lost his mind. He shook his head, blinked a few times, then said, "If you want to know the truth, it was the publisher's decision. I had nothing to do with it."

Zac threw his head back and scoffed. "You really expect me to believe that?"

"I don't care what you believe. It's the truth."

"Boys!" Nikki said, breaking in. "You haven't even touched your drinks yet. How about we toast to good old times? What do you say?"

Zac and Finn looked at each other. They looked at their VBs.

It couldn't be denied. The amber fluid was beckoning them from old times. They slowly picked up their glasses and, somewhat robotically, held them high. Nikki raised her glass of wine and clinked them both with gusto. "Tchin tchin!"

They each took a sip and let the moment ride.

Finn, feeling an overwhelming sense of guilt, but refusing to acknowledge it, put his glass down and said, "If it's any consolation, I'm not going to ask what you thought of my book. You can write it off as commercial fiction and assume it's crap."

"*Your* book," Zac said disparagingly, putting his glass down.

"Your name's in the acknowledgement section—for posterity," Finn said with half-veiled sarcasm.

"I saw it—along with your hollow claim that you ought to be considered a ghost writer, rather than a real author."

"I insisted on it against my publisher's advice."

Zac rolled his eyes. "But you didn't insist on shared royalties, did you?"

Finn shook his head. "That's not true. The publisher left it to my discretion."

"And?"

"We can split the royalties if you want."

"That's your offer?"

Finn let out an exasperated sigh. "I'm being generous mate!"

"How about I talk to a lawyer about it?"

Finn's frustration flared. "There's no need for that mate!"

"Stop calling me mate. I'm not your friend anymore."

Nikki intervened again. "Boys, please! Why don't we settle it like gentlemen?"

"Like gentlemen," Zac echoed.

"Yes," Nikki said, shrugging her shoulders nonchalantly, as if to say, *why not?*

Maintaining the initiative, Zac said, "So how do you propose we settle it then? It's not like we're lawyers, or politicians, or diplomats. We're writers. Or at least some of us are."

"How flattering of you," Finn said unamused.

"My pleasure," Zac said, pretending not to care.

"Gentlemen," Nikki said, "I appreciate your détente, but let's think about what's more important here. The art, right? You're all ego. It seems you've forgotten that Art is your mistress. Without her, you're nothing. You're nobody. Not all the money and fame in the world will make you happy—if you disrespect her."

Finn and Zac looked at her, speechless. It was like she had transformed, before their very eyes, into Athena, and they were forced to shield themselves from the blinding light that radiated out of her.

Seeing the effect she had on them, she gave them the sweetest smile that any woman could ever give, without taking sides, which was quite an achievement, because she genuinely found it difficult to decide which of the two was more authentic. She had the feeling that the question wasn't going to be easily answered— at least not intellectually. So she came up with an idea. She didn't say it out loud right away. She allowed herself a private moment to savor the pleasure of it. "I think ..." she said, baiting them, "that you should debate it fairly, each one giving the other a chance to speak, and then we'll judge who is right."

"You mean you will judge," Finn said right away.

"Sure, why not?"

Finn looked at Zac, who, evidently had already decided.

"It's a good idea," he agreed. "In fact, why don't we make a bet."

"A bet?" Finn said, openly expressing distaste at the idea.

"Yeah. Whoever delivers the best argument takes the lion's share of the royalties."

"You're joking, right?"

"No."

Finn looked at Nikki, hoping she would come to his defense. But she shocked him by saying: "I think it's a good idea. The higher the stakes, the harder you both have to work to prove your point."

Zac nodded sagely at hearing this.

Finn, feeling himself knot up, reached for his beer and chugged down half the glass.

Nikki and Zac watched him and grinned.

When Finn didn't say anything, Zac said, "Well, what do you say?"

Finn wiped his lips. "You guys are really serious about this?"

Nikki and Zac said, "Yep!"

Peeved that Zac and Nikki seemed to be colluding against him, Finn said, "In that case there has to be some rules, to make it fair. A time limit, an opportunity for rebuttal, that sort of thing."

"Agreed," Zac said, "just like debating class."

Nikki nodded in agreement.

Zac said, "Three minutes for openers, three for rebuttal and one for a closing. How does that sound?"

Finn chewed his lip, thought about it for a moment, then said, "Ok."

Zac clapped his hands and said, "Excellent! This is going to be fun!"

Nikki intervened, however. Her expression that was halfway between serious and mischievous. She said, "Not so fast! We've still got to decide on a topic. It seems to me that we're talking about theft, right?"

"Theft?" Finn said, unsure.

"Yes. Theft of art to be exact," Nikki added.

Zac slapped his hand down on the table. "I like it!"

Nikki said, "I'm not finished yet."

Zac's enthusiasm immediately evaporated.

"We have to honour Art, and so each of you has to take the other's side."

"What do you mean by that?" Zac asked.

"What I mean is, you Zac, you have to argue that 'All art is not theft,' and you Finn, you have to argue the opposite."

"I have to argue that 'All art is theft'?" Finn said, practically choking on the idea.

"You got it."

Zac shook his head in wonder at Nikki. He was liking this girl more each minute!

"So if I had to start somewhere," Zac began, "it would have to be with a story. Let me introduce exhibit A: Shakespeare's *Romeo and Juliet*. How many times has it been re-done? Did Shakespeare invent it? Maybe he copied it from somewhere. Or, maybe the idea lives somewhere in the ether. In which, case no one owns it because it's everyone's. Let me give you an example: *West Side Story*. The story begins in the late 1940s when Montgomery Clift suggested the idea to Jerry Robbins—you have to excuse me if I get into some detail here, it's the details that count, they prove my point—so Robbins liked the idea and took it to Leonard Bernstein. Bernstein would later recall that Robbins came to him with "a noble idea." Now isn't that interesting? Was it because the idea was based on Shakespeare, or was it because the idea had its own life? I'll let you be the judge of that. So what was the idea? This is where it gets intriguing, because the first version they came up with was Tony playing a Jew, and Maria playing an Irish Catholic—you know—for roles of Romeo and Juliet. Some people have it the other way around, but if you read Arthur Laurent's account, the guy who actually wrote the script, that's how it was." Zac looked at Nikki and Finn to make sure they were following. He could tell they weren't, so he said, "Arthur Laurent came on board as the writer. His job was to turn Robbin's and Bernstein's idea into words. Since we're talking about writing, he's the man we'll be following. So ... it turned out that everyone was busy and the project was shelved. But then in 1955, Laurent happened to run into Bernstein again—I think it was in Los Angeles. They were hanging out in Beverly Hills, by this pool apparently, munching on club sandwiches amongst the glamour, and it just so happened that they got talking about the gang riots that happened the night before, reported in the newspapers, and it struck them that they could take Robbin's original idea and reshape it as a story between two lovers from opposite gangs. And that is how Laurent's original idea became *West Side Story*. Tony was cast as an Irish Catholic and Maria as a Puerto Rican, and it was set in Spanish Harlem."

He looked at Nikki and Finn for a reaction. He could see that their minds were ticking over.

"I suppose you want to know how *West Side Story* wasn't stolen from *Romeo and Juliet*?" Finn asked.

Zac said, "Well, according to Laurent, when they played it in London—where people supposedly really knew their Shakespeare—they commented on the fact that Juliet's message didn't get through because of the plague—if you remember, there's a scene where Friar John is sent to deliver the message to Romeo about Juliet's faux death. But the Friar is suspected of having been in an infected house and is quarantined, making him unable to deliver the message to Romeo, which leads to the tragedy. In *West Side Story*, the message of love fails to get through not because of a plague, but because of bigotry and violence. So this is an original re-mapping of the critical scene. And the London audiences received it really well."

"So *West Side Story* wasn't stolen because ..." Nikki said, holding out her hands, palm open.

"Because imagine that *West Side Story* was written first," Zac said. "Shakespeare could have taken it and set it between two feuding Italian families during the plague, and that would have been his version. But that isn't what matters. What matters is that lovers crossing social boundaries is a theme that is as old as our species." And to prove his point, he added, "What's the odds that at some distant point in our past a love-struck Neanderthal fell in love with a fair-haired Homo sapien maiden? I know it's a radical suggestion, but if you think about it, the odds have to be on it. I mean, all you have to do is look at some of the meat heads in our society, the way they walk around with their knuckles dragging on the ground while they scan the world like dumb brutes from under heavy brow ridges."

"You've got no argument from me," Nikki said.

Finn was shaking his head with a sour expression on his face, like he knew he had no chance of winning this debate.

Nikki was grinning happily. "Come on," she said, prodding him with her elbow. "You can do it."

Finn smirked. "Well, if you're going to argue about Neanderthals, then I guess I'll have to defend them," he said," trying to sound flippant.

"Hit me with your best shot," Zac replied.

"I know of cave art," Finn began. "Let's assume it was done by Neanderthals. If not, then by their contemporaries—I don't know, Cro Magnon Man I believe. It's the earliest figurative art on record. That ought to make it original, right?" He looked at Nikki and Zac, seeking their approval.

Nikki and Zac nodded, letting him know that he should continue.

"But what does 'original' mean? The kinds of things they painted—lions, antelope, horses, I don't know, wart hogs, who knows—they copied them from nature. They effectively stole nature's ideas. They didn't invent the lion. The lion was invented by nature."

"Is that your argument? Zac asked.

"Wait on," Finn said. "There's more."

"Ok."

"If you think about it, what is stealing? It's depriving someone of property. Like if I steal a farmer's cow, he is going to lose productivity. Maybe even a friend. It directly impacts his life. But what is stolen when someone takes another person's artistic idea? What are they being deprived of? It's not very clear. Is it the potential for future profitability? If we take that as our interpretation, does it logically follow that we ought to place a cause-and-effect relationship between the artistic idea and the money it generates? If true, does the amount of money that an art object generates equate to the value of the idea itself? If you think about it, this assumes that the artist has been able to perfectly transfer their idea from their head to the physical world. Is this actually possible? Maybe it doesn't matter. But it seems to me that if anything is stolen, it's something more than just the idea. Let's call it the intention of the idea. In that case, I stole the idea that Zac aspired to, not the actual idea itself. The actual idea ... well, it's hard to say where that exists." He looked at Zac and Nikki, saw that they were having doubts. In an effort to preempt them, he said, "I admit an idea is something that exists inside our heads. But I wonder if it exists out in nature as well. By which I mean ... it might not have a name like we put on it, but its potentiality exists in the form of information. You get what I'm saying?"

Nikki looked at Zac. Zac seemed to understand, but he wasn't forthcoming.

Finn had had seen this before. How many times had they argued about stuff just like this? And then it hit him. He remembered something he had read somewhere. He snapped his fingers excitedly and said, "I've got it! Think of DNA. Right? it carries information. Right?"

Zac and Nikki nodded in unison.

Emboldened, he said, "But DNA is not the whole story." He could see them starting to balk. He ignored them and went on. "It turns out that DNA has switches. It's the switches that determine how DNA is expressed. You can have two identical sets of DNA, but if the switches are different, then the outcome will be completely different. The same applies to art. The idea behind a work of art is its DNA. You can steal that. Yes! But the switches—

that depends on the artists. Two different artists will have two different sets of—"

"—Switches!" Nikki interjected enthusiastically—much to Zac's annoyance.

"Exactly!" Finn exalted.

Zac wasn't happy, but he acknowledged the argument.

Nikki didn't care. She patted her hands and said, "Bravo! Bravo!"

Zac forced smile.

Sensing his taciturn state, Nikki turned to him and said, "Rebuttal?"

Zac slowly gathered himself together and said, "It's true, I never discussed the specific intention behind *My Secret Disease*, but," and he addressed Finn directly, "you knew the entire reason why I created the story in the first place—the DNA of the idea if you want to call it that— was to prove that literary fiction is a 'toad dressed in pyjamas.'"

Nikki gave Zac a funny look. "A toad dressed in pyjamas?"

"That's putting it nicely," Zac said.

"I'm not sure if I understand what you mean," she said.

Finn looked at Zac, then at Nikki. "It's personal joke. You don't have to get it."

Nikki was adamant. "But I want to understand."

Finn sighed. "Have you heard the expression 'Paper Tiger'?"

"Oh, yeah, right, I know that one."

"Although it's a little more subtle than that, because in this case we're talking about a toad dressed in a tuxedo. So it's an extension of the idea, because pyjamas in this case refers to privilege and wealth," Finn explained.

Nikki giggled and struck a pose. "I've modelled designer loungewear before. I know the market."

"But it still doesn't weaken my point," Finn said to Zac, "because I aimed *My Secret Disease* at the commercial market, which you clearly despise."

"How about I take it to a lawyer and see what they say?" Zac said simply.

"You don't have to do that," Finn said firmly.

"I don't?"

"No. We can settle this like gentlemen."

"Then I want at least fifty-one percent of the profits."

"Fifty-one percent? You didn't write a word of it. You just gave me the idea."

"And the idea is worth the controlling share."

Finn looked at Nikki for support. "Do you think he deserves that?"

For the first time, Nikki appeared to squirm. "I can't make that decision," she said. "I haven't read it, I don't know how much you wrote, how much Zac wrote—"

"—He didn't write anything," Finn blurted, getting emotionally agitated.

"I meant how much of his idea influenced you," Nikki said firmly, holding her ground.

The veins on Zac's temples were starting to bulge. "I'll tell you how much my idea influenced him," he said with a strained voice. "It was very detailed, it outlined the entire plot, the psychological stakes, everything. All he had to do was join the dots."

"Is that all you think I did?" Finn said, his voice rising in anger.

Nikki opened her mouth to speak, but Zac silenced her. "I'll tell you right now. The only chapter that you did a reasonable job on was Wilford's last victim—and that's because I gave it to you verbatim. Every other chapter was fake. You tried to emulate the style, but it lacks substance. It's a conman trying to impress a mark."

"Huh!" Finn said, deeply offended. "And if you wrote it? It would have turned into another one of your self-hating diatribes!"

Nikki stood up. "I don't have to listen to this," she said, and grabbed her bag.

Finn looked at her with a forlorn expression.

Zac's face had turned to stone.

Nikki said, "Goodbye," and walked off.

"Wait!" Finn said, and rushed after her.

Nikki headed for the exit.

Finn ran up to her and said, "I'm sorry. Don't go."

Nikki turned to him with some anger of her own, and said, "Don't you think it's a little too late for that?"

Finn looked into her eyes, and knew she was serious. "Let me take you to where you want to go," he pleaded.

Nikki said, "I can find my own way, thank-you very much," and pushed the door open and walked out into the late afternoon sun.

Finn continued following her. "Look, I don't blame you. I was an idiot in there. Just think for a moment, would you have done any better in that situation?"

"I wouldn't have stolen his idea in the first place," she said, walking briskly down the street without knowing where she was going.

"Really?" Finn said, "and I thought Europeans had that down to a fine art."

Nikki didn't say anything. She kept on walking.

Finn kept pace with her and said, "Where are you going?"

"Anywhere without you."

Finn pretended to ignore her. They kept on walking, Nikki making no attempt to eject Finn from her personal space.

They reached the corner of Queen and Oxford, it was a big intersection. Nikki's eyes darted around, looking for what Finn presumed was a taxi.

"Let me drive you," he insisted.

They stood like that for a while, while the cars whizzed by.

When no taxis came, Nikki looked up at the sky and swore something in French.

Finn said, "You're not going to get a taxi here. Let me drive you."

She turned to him and became visibly anguished. "Why do I

always fall for egotistical fucks?"

Finn tried to hide his reaction. He straightened up and said, "You deserve better than that."

She gave him a sarcastic look and mumbled something else in French he didn't understand.

He said, "Come on. We can put this behind us."

She seemed to ignore him. She looked past him.

Zac was standing outside the Light Brigade Hotel on the pavement, looking at them.

"But you'll never put him behind you, will you?" she said, looking at Zac.

Finn looked at Zac and a flicker of a grimace passed across his face.

Zac didn't respond.

Finn looked at Nikki again. He didn't want to let her go. It wasn't just her looks. It was the energy she radiated. He felt like they had met for a reason. "I tell you what. I've got an idea," he said. "Come on."

Nikki expressed uncertainty.

Finn said, "There was something I wanted to tell you earlier, but we got so carried away I forgot."

Nikki's eyes narrowed ever so slightly.

"I'm having a big party at my place this Saturday, to celebrate the book. Everyone will be there. What do you say I invite Zac?"

Nikki returned her gaze to Zac in the distance. She held it there for quite some time before answering. "You think he'll accept?"

"He has to. Important people will be there who can help his career. He'd be a fool not to come."

"What makes you think I'll come?"

Finn broke into a smile for time since walking out. "You definitely do not want to miss out on seeing my parent's house."

– 21 –
Ali Baba's

Zac met Leila in the back lane. She came out through the fly-wire door, closing it quietly behind her, wary, like a caged animal that had just been set free.

"You came back," she said, stopping a short distance from him. She was in genuine disbelief.

"Yes."

"You could have written and told me, instead of surprising me like this."

"I'm sorry. I surprised even myself."

She cast a furtive glance back into the kitchen through the fly screen. "If you had told me, I could have taken the night off."

"It's okay. I won't keep you long."

They stared at each other in silence. Leila was fascinated with his beard. She thought he had aged immensely. Perhaps it was in his eyes, which were dark and liquid, full of hidden meanings that she ached to know about.

He stepped a little closer and said, "I got your letter."

"And?"

"I was very moved by it."

"Is that why you came back?"

He flicked his eyes away for a fleeting moment and she knew that it wasn't.

He reached out his hand to her and she stepped back.

He retracted his hand. Took stock of himself. "We need to talk," he said.

"Talk then."

"No, I mean later. When you get off."

"What makes you think I want to wait around?"

"Leila, please ..."

She shook her head with a heavy sadness. "I thought ..."

"You are right," he said quickly, filling the empty space.

"Right about what?"

"About us."

"I thought you said there is no 'us.'"

"No, no ... there is an us. And it's special."

"But you're leaving again."

He looked down, kicked the ground with his shoe. "I don't know about that yet. It depends."

"Depends on what?"

"On a whole lot of things. That's what we need to talk about."

Leila studied his eyes. They seemed to be speaking a secret language that eluded her. Should she dare hope? She hated second guessing herself like this. She wished he just came right out and say it. But an invisible force-field had inserted itself between them. "You know I don't get off till one a.m."

"I know."

"I'll have to sneak downstairs after everyone's gone to sleep."

"I know."

She sighed. But behind it her heart was pounding like drum.

He slowly backed away, his eyes staying on her, until his face slipped into the shadows.

Zac was waiting in his car at the end of the block when Leila came home with her mum and dad. Her father, Maroun, was a solid-looking man, with meaty arms and a proud chest. He had a paunch, but it suited him. Made him look like an authentic restaurateur. He let the women go into the house while he stood outside for a while smoking a cigarette.

Zac wouldn't say he was afraid of Maroun. He respected him fully. More than once though, Maroun had made it abundantly clear that Leila was a good girl and deserved better than a wanna-be writer dish-hand. Zac didn't disagree.

But he also wanted to prove him wrong.

Right now, though, wasn't the time or place for it. He stayed in the shadows until Maroun finished his cigarette and went inside.

He waited almost another half hour before the upstairs lights went off. He was alone with his thoughts now. In the shadowy light, an image rose up in his consciousness. He saw himself as a buried monument from a distant civilization. The hot sands abrasively smoothing off the rough edges. The hollowed-out eyes staring into space, speaking mysteries that reached back in time. He needed to wake up. Become human again.

He looked up and saw her coming down the front steps and swing the wrought iron gate. She stopped, looked left and right. He opened his door. She snapped her eyes one him like a vigilant bird.

She hovered there for a moment. Then briskly walked towards his car and got in.

They sat in silence for a while, listened to each other's breathing.

"It's still warm," she said quietly, breaking the silence. She didn't look at him; she kept looking straight ahead.

"Yes,' he replied. It was almost a whisper.

"So what are we doing here?" she asked still holding her gaze.

"A friend of mine ... he published a book."

She turned to him, looked at him from afar. "So that's why you came back?"

"If you let me explain ..."

"If I wrote something, if I published ..." she mused. "But then it wouldn't be because of me, would it?"

"I wanted to see you. I didn't want to see him."

She momentarily held her breath in anticipation.

"He stole my idea. I came down to confront him about it."

"He stole your idea?"

He turned to face her fully. "It's called My Secret Disease."

"Oh ..."

"You know about it?"

"I saw it in a bookstore window."

"Well, he stole my idea."

"He stole your idea." She said it much more slowly this time, weighing it up for real.

"Yeah."

"You'll have to explain."

Zac collected his thoughts. "We were friends. We met at university. He's a rich kid. A spoiled brat. His father made him do economics and stuff, but he wanted to be a writer."

Leila began softly laughing.

"What?"

"Everyone wants to be a writer."

Zac nodded humourlessly. "But only few succeed. Money helps."

"What about talent?"

"Talent ..."

"Yeah. The magic spark."

Zac sighed. "It's true. Anyone can be a writer. I suppose that's why Finn published and I'm still in the wilderness."

Leila put out a hand and laid it on Zac's forearm. "Your time will come."

"I think my time is passed."

Leila lifted her hand and slapped down hard. "Don't say that!"

He sucked in a deep breath, let it out again.

"It's never too late. If you love writing, it's like breathing. There's no end until it ends."

"Is that what your poet tells you?"

"No, I made it up myself."

"You're talented, you realize that?"

For an instant, Leila felt like she wanted to believe that with every fiber of her being. But then she gave a self-deprecating laugh. "Your messing with me."

"No, I'm being real."

Leila still didn't believe him. As much as she would have liked to bottle his words, carry them around with her, uncork them every now and then and sniff the odor of big dreams ... she wouldn't allow herself to do that. It wasn't who she was. She came from the inside. Like a seed. She might be sprouting. But she knew that there was an infinite amount of growing to do. She shook her head. "We both know that talent is not enough. You need to be a genius, and even then you still need to have luck on your side."

"Finn got lucky."

"Maybe because he stole your luck."

"Maybe."

"So you're telling me his book—his entire book—was your

idea?"

"Practically."

"That's a big claim."

"I gave him a complete synopsis."

"I see. Have you thought about going to a lawyer?"

"I don't have the money."

"What about going to the newspapers."

"I've thought about it."

"Do it."

He mulled the thought over. "He invited me to party on Saturday. To celebrate the success of his book."

Leila took a moment to process that. "Are you going to go?"

"There'll be lots of industry people there, other writers ... he said he would introduce me to his editor."

"Wow! That's ..."

"I know."

Leila quickly made up her mind. "You have to go."

"I suppose so."

"No, really, you have to go."

"He said, 'bring someone along.'"

"Really?"

"Yeah."

"Who were you thinking of?"

"That's a stupid question."

Leila felt herself blush. "You mean it?"

"I wouldn't have said it if I didn't mean it."

– 22 –
Point Piper

"**D**ID you bring the gear?" Finn asked in a hushed voice.

Zac barely heard the question. Nikki distracted him as she breezed across the step to greet Leila. Leila had been standing stiffly behind Zac, holding her crossbody handbag in front of her as a protective shield. Nikki's effusive praise for Leila's dress—a lilac midi—seemed to make Leila relax a little and she allowed herself a demure, if slightly bewildered smile. Nikki for her part was wearing a robin's-egg blue cocktail dress with a plunging neckline that left little to the imagination.

"Zac?" Finn reminded him.

"Oh yeah." He snapped out of his daydream and patted his back pocket. "I got it."

The women didn't seem to notice. Nikki was talking at a hundred miles an hour and took Leila's hand and whisked her into the party.

Zac followed Finn inside. The sound of jazz music mingled with voices and laughter floated down the hallway as they made their way into the kitchen.

"This is Gerard," Finn said, to a red-headed gentleman dressed in a tuxedo serving cocktails over the breakfast bar.

Gerard saluted his new guests and asked them what they wanted to drink. A cluster of people stood at the threshold of the kitchen and looked on, holding drinks while they chatted amongst themselves.

Leila said, "Can you make a Pomegranate martini?"

Gerard smiled and said, "That's very exotic. We don't have pomegranates, but I have strawberries. Will those do?"

"Yes, that's fine, thank-you," Leila said, not wanting to make a fuss.

Gerard mixed Leila's cocktail, macerated some strawberries, added them and passed it to her. As he did so, he asked Zac what he would like to drink.

Zac said, "A four ex if you've got it."

Gerard smiled again and said, "Sorry we don't carry those, but if you'd like, we have Victoria Bitter, or Corona in long necks."

"Corona then."

"Excellent choice." Gerard reached down into a tub of ice and pulled out a Corona.

Finn grabbed a Corona as well and directed Zac and Leila

across the lounge room, which was packed with people, and out onto the patio, where Evelyn was hanging out with Kenji. Along the way, Nikki got waylaid by someone and she peeled off.

Evelyn and Kenji were engaged in conversation, but as soon as Finn appeared with Zac and Leila, they paused and diverted all their attention to the newcomers.

Finn said, "Guess who?"

Evelyn jerked a bemused little smile and said, "The Zac Levin I presume?" It was obvious she was a little tipsy. She held a flute of champagne in one hand and a cigarette in the other. She transferred her glass and cigarette to her left hand and theatrically struck her right hand out at him.

"This is he," Zac said, shaking her hand with a flourish.

Finn chuckled at the display.

"And your lady friend?" Evelyn asked, noticing Leila was holding herself in reserve.

Leila introduced herself.

"As in the song," Evelyn said.

"As in the song," Leila replied, "except spelt differently."

"A very important distinction," Evelyn said.

"I hope so," Leila said.

Evelyn let out a throaty laugh.

"I'm Kenji," Kenji said, introducing himself.

Zac and Leila politely greeted him.

Finn nudged Zac and said, "Do you mind?" He flicked his eyes to the stairs that led down to his bedroom.

Zac said, "Oh yeah," and made to move, but Evelyn had begun asking him a question. He stopped.

Evelyn said, "I'd be interested to hear what sort of stuff you write."

Zac's mouth twitched into a half-smile, his eyes glazing over with a distant look, as if the question was like asking how to catch air with a net.

Evelyn took a drag of her cigarette and blew the air upwards, into the sky. She leveled her eyes on him, letting him know he wasn't going to escape so easily.

Zac imperceptibly nodded. An acknowledgment that he had better come up with something convincing. "Let me put it this way," he said. "At university they crushed us under the weight of literary history, then threw they us in the ocean to see if we would sink or swim."

"So which one was you?"

"Right now?"

"Today, tomorrow ..."

"Right now, the sharks are circling."

Evelyn liked that. "So you're looking for someone to pull you out of the water?"

Zac gave her a knowing smile. "That wouldn't be heroic, would it? Nah, I'm just waiting for the right current to come along. Maybe I've found it."

"Pray tell," Evelyn said, belying a soft belly under her practiced carapace.

"I would," Zac said, but Finn was tugging on his arm. "Later?"

"Later," she echoed, her tone carrying an edge of amusement — and challenge. "But don't keep me waiting too long, Zac. Currents have a way of sweeping you out to sea if you're not careful."

Zac turned his head slightly and grinned at her from the corner of his eye, the game of wit as familiar to him as an old tune, but he was feeling out of practice, and with Finn dragging on his arm, he welcomed the chance to retreat from the spotlight before his rhythm faltered.

As they descended the steps to Finn's bedroom, Finn said, "What was all that about? You two know each other?"

"I've never met her in my life."

"You could have fooled me."

Finn opened the door to his bedroom and let Zac inside. He closed the door behind them.

Zac pulled a zip-lock bag from his rear pocket and held it up for Finn to see.

Finn took it, unzipped it, wet his finger and tasted it. "Good shit mate!"

"Quality is my middle name."

"Fuck yeah!" He put the baggy on his desk, got out his wallet, drew a ten-buck note and smoothed it out. There was book with a glossy hardcover: The Virgin Suicides. He formed the ten-buck note into a half pipe and scooped out some cocaine then tapped it onto the book cover. He formed four rows, rolled up the note and snorted two in quick succession. "Woah!" He passed the note to Zac.

Zac hesitated. "I don't normally partake," he said.

"Come on mate!" Finn said. "For old time's sake."

Zac reluctantly took the note and snorted the remaining two lines.

Finn looked at Zac's response. "Yeah?"

Zac pulled a stoic face. "Yeah."

"Come on," Finn said. "Let's party!"

They returned to the party, floating through the swirls and eddies of human flesh.

Finn pushed ahead and Zac slowed down, until the Finn was gone and Zac was left alone amongst strangers. The music had changed to a pulsating grunge. Someone had put Nirvana's In Utero on. The room was swaying hypnotically to "Heart-Shaped Box."

Zac got caught up in it and he started swayed along with the others. He felt like he had become part of one big organism. The smell of marijuana wafted on the air. A girl in brown corduroys with sewn-on sunflower patches and a floral top began dancing with him. Zac obliged.

Finn found Nikki talking to one of Finn's old friends from his writer's group in Bronte. Charlie had a thick bushy beard, pot belly, and looked like a sloth. His droopy eyes, however, betrayed a formidable knowledge of medieval history. He employed it to write historical fiction, usually about a hero chasing a relic that involved saving a maiden or two along the way.

Finn pulled Nikki away and took her down to his room, set up a couple of lines for her.

They came out just as Leila was heading down to the toilet annexed to the laundry.

They smiled at each other in passing.

Leila was thinking about the conversation she had shared with Evelyn and Kenji after Zac and Finn left her alone. She found Kenji to be extremely interesting. It was the first time she had had a conversation with a Japanese man apart from the limited contact she had with Japanese people at her father's restaurant. She had certainly never met a *manga* artist before.

He told her about his love of drawing and how it enabled him to "be himself." Evelyn said that was the best anyone could expect as an artist. It was a dog-eat-dog world out there, and if you enjoyed what you did—even if it didn't pay the rent—you were already better off than half the world who spent half their lives stuck in traffic jams, trudging to menial, meaningless jobs that ground them down into zombies.

Leila told them she was stuck in her father's restaurant.

That drew "oohs and aahs" of sympathy from Evelyn and Kenji.

It was at this juncture that she decided to tell them about her desire to become a writer. Her fear, in that moment, was that they would think she was just another dreamer who was paying lip service to the idea, rather than a genuine devotee of the art.

She was only too painfully aware of the cancer that had infected her generation, the disillusionment and moral decay that many wore with a badge of pride. She thanked her lucky stars that she kept her virginity and didn't lose it like one of her friends who had gotten plastered with alcohol and got fucked by multiple men while in a semi-comatose state. Nor did she imagine that she might one day find a knight in shining armour who would undress her gently, kiss her softly in all the right places, then house her in a luxurious castle with manicured gardens. No, she wanted something else. Something sharp-edged and real. She wanted to touch the raw seam between life and death, to catch the moment where existence teetered on its precipice and trap it in words, if she could. As much as she followed her parent's religion, she didn't believe in the afterlife. It smacked of delusion, and she was a realist. But the people standing in front of her wouldn't know that. They would see a naive Lebanese girl with homely features smiling shyly at them, nervous with stage-fright. But somehow, somewhere in between having these thoughts and looking ahead, thinking, she heard herself say: "But I want to become a writer!"

Evelyn's face contorted into a humorous smirk, which lasted just long enough for Leila to slump into an angry frown.

"Sorry," Evelyn said. "It's not surprised you said it. It's just the way you said it."

"Was I being too serious?" Leila asked.

"Truth be told, we're all cynical to the point of being mummified," Evelyn replied jokingly.

Kenji said, "Mummified?"

Evelyn said, "The ancient Egyptian art of preserving cadavers."

"Cadavers?"

"Rotting dead bodies."

"Ah."

Evelyn's comment clarified something Leila already felt. If you want to be in this business, be prepared to go to Hell and back. The woman standing in front of her certainly epitomized it. She could have been the walking dead. Someone had drunk her blood. Paid the price. It got her thinking: "We're all searching for something, even while we pretend life is meaningless."

"Ooh, that's deep," Evelyn said.

Kenji's eyes lit up and he said, "In Japan we think the exact opposite! We call it mono no aware. But don't ask me to explain it. It's too difficult."

"Mono no aware," Leila said. "I like it. Could you try?"

Kenji scratched his head, tilting it to the side. "Yah—I'm not sure. If I had to ..."

Leila encouraged him with a gentle: "Go on."

"I suppose ... sadness is the word that comes to mind."

"Sadness?"

"Yes. Sadness knowing that life is short, but beautiful, like a flower that opens its petals for a few days then decays."

"So you're saying, cherish the moment even while it is already passing?"

"Something like that."

Evelyn had listened to this without expression. Her cigarette was at its end. She took one last drag on it then leaned forward and crushed it out in an ash tray on a small round table nearby.

"If that's true, then I think I'd like to visit Japan," Leila said.

"Please do," Kenji said. "You'll love it."

"I've never been to Japan," Evelyn said. "Can you recommend anywhere worth visiting?"

"Oh boy! There are so many places. It depends on what you like. What do you like?"

Evelyn thought about it for a moment and said, "I've heard that they have some beautiful gardens."

"Oh yeah. They do. In that case, you should visit Kyoto. It has some of the most beautiful gardens in Japan. Personally, though, I prefer the cemeteries." He smiled cheekily.

"Cemeteries?" Leila asked.

"Yeah. They're full of history and they have a fantastic atmosphere. I love walking through them imagining all the people that once lived."

"Interesting," Evelyn said.

"Is that where you get your inspiration from?" Leila asked.

"Sometimes, yes."

"What kind of drawings do you do?"

Kenji smiled. Having been asked this question many times, he was well-practiced by now. "I am currently exploring spirit transformation," he said confidently.

"Spirit transformation," Leila said.

"Think of it this way," Kenji said. "A machine blends into a human. Or an animal become part human. That sort of thing."

Evelyn said, "That's wild. Are you saying machines have a spirit?"

"Of course," Kenji replied. "In Japan, everything has a spirit."

"How does that work?" Leila asked.

Kenji grinned like monkey. "Don't ask me. I have no idea. I just like drawing weird things."

That got Evelyn and Leila laughing.

No meaning to be impolite, Leila said, "I'd like to continue this conversation. But I need to go to the bathroom. Do you know where it is?"

Evelyn pointed over the crowd of dancers: "I believe it's that way."

On her way back from the toilet, Leila stopped outside Finn's bedroom. When Finn and Nikki had come out earlier, they were sporting mischievous smiles, hinting at some hanky-panky that had transpired. She wasn't sure why, but she was seized by a pang of curiosity. Before she could second-guess herself, she turned the doorknob and stepped inside. She lingered for a moment, then quietly shut the door behind her.

Her eyes were immediately drawn to the view of Sydney Harbour, framed by north-facing floor-to-ceiling windows. A neatly trimmed hedge interrupted the view, but not enough to obscure the green patch she recognized as Taronga Zoo across the other side. In front of the windows sat a queen-sized bed, unmade and slightly disheveled—the doona bunched into one corner, the crinkled sheets pulled askew, carrying a faint scent of sweat and perfume.

Next to the bed stood a small side table topped with an Art Nouveau lamp. Several dog-eared paperbacks were stacked haphazardly on top of one another, the topmost being Rising Sun by Michael Crichton. On the other side of the bed was a door leading to an en-suite bathroom. Leila peeked inside. It was tiled white, had a large shower area—big enough for two—and had plush used towels draped over a wooden rack.

Along the opposite wall stood a bookshelf. The glass doors on the lower section were crammed with an eclectic collection of volumes. Classics like The Great Gatsby shared space with cheap crime paperbacks and esoteric philosophy texts. On the upper shelves, a cluster of surfing trophies gleamed under the light—an ostentatious reminder of a privileged adolescence.

And then there was the desk—a battered wooden antique, its wear and tear suggesting both age and value. Atop it sat an old Corona typewriter, flanked by piles of paper and even more books. One particular book caught her attention—a glossy hardcover that gleamed with faint smudges. She stepped closer, swiped her finger across its surface and inspected the result—so that explained it.

But her attention was quickly diverted. Among the papers,

she spotted a paper-clipped sheaf with the heading: 'Burning Ambitions.' She picked it up and started reading:

Brief plot outline:

In modern-day Japan, a disgruntled *manga* artist, Hajime Sano, convinced his ideas were stolen by his former boss, burns down a renowned manga art house in an act of vengeance. The devastating incident leaves him sentenced to death, a fate he awaits in isolation.

Enter Emiko Tanaka, a young *manga* artist shaken after her own creative concepts were seemingly stolen following a discussion at a comic convention. The experience leaves her disillusioned, grappling with the fragility of artistic ownership and the vulnerability of sharing her work. Drawn to Hajime's story, she begins corresponding with him in prison, believing he understands her pain and frustration.

Through their letters, an unexpected bond forms, grounded in shared doubts and unspoken fears. Hajime, initially unrepentant, reveals how his belief in the theft of his work consumed him, fueling a spiral of bitterness and destruction. Yet as he reflects on his life, doubts creep in: were his ideas truly stolen, or were they simply a product of the cultural zeitgeist, echoes of the collective creative consciousness? His uncertainty unsettles Emiko. She begins to question her own experience—were her ideas as original as she believed, or were they also shaped by the endless flow of shared influences?

The more they write, the more she sees herself in his delusion. She recalls moments where she, too, borrowed inspiration—consciously or unconsciously—from the world around her. She realizes how the ego, with its hunger for validation, had blinded her to the fluid and interconnected nature of creativity. Art, she comes to understand, is less a solitary act of ownership and more a shared language shaped by countless voices over time.

As their connection deepens, they make the unconventional decision to have a "spiritual marriage," a symbolic union to honor their shared quest for understanding and redemption. For Hajime, it is a final gesture of atonement. For Emiko, it is a vow to move beyond ego-driven pain and embrace humility in her art.

When his execution finally comes, Emiko fulfills his last wish: to scatter his ashes over the waters in Kamakura, under the serene gaze of the Great Buddha at *Kōtoku-in*. Standing there, she lets the ashes fall, her hands trembling with the weight of his mistake, his delusion, his sin. She silently prays for his spirit's release and for her own clarity of purpose.

As the waves carry his ashes away, she makes a solemn vow: never to fall into the same ego trap that consumed him. She will honor the collective nature of creation, protect her voice without succumbing to possessiveness, and move forward with grace and gratitude for the shared tapestry of art. Walking away from the shore, she feels lighter, the burden of bitterness replaced by the resolve to create with an open heart.

Full synopsis—

The door handle clicked. Leila jolted in panic. Without think-ing, she hurriedly stuffed the notes into her bag just as Finn and a couple of strangers came in.

"Oh, I didn't expect you to be in here," Finn remarked.

"I'm sorry, the other toilet was occupied. I found a toilet in here ..."

"Oh, I see. No problems."

"Thanks," Leila said, and she quickly left the room.

She kept hurrying until she reached the top of the stairs, and stopped. Her eyes immediately fixed on Zac, who, much to Lei-la's consternation was dancing with Nikki. Not just dancing, but sharing the same bubble. Nikki's arms were draped over his shoulders and her eyes were seductively caressing his face. A se-ries of flashes went off in Leila's head. A momentary tsunami of giddiness overwhelmed her. She had to reach out and clasp the handrail to steady herself. It quickly passed and was replaced by the white-hot heat of jealousy and anger. She made an un-feminine-like guttural sound, then pushed her way through the crowd to the kitchen and stomped down the hallway and out of the house.

Zac caught her from the corner of his eye, broke away from Nikki and fought his way through the crowd after her.

Leila was already marching up the street. Zac chased her and grabbed her right arm.

Leila swung around and violently pulled away. "Don't touch me!"

Zac withdrew. He stared at her with a mixture of incredulity and hurt.

Leila momentarily averted her eyes; she refused to see what she saw. She turned away and resumed her march up the street.

Zac shadowed her. "Surely you're bigger than this?" he said, half angry, half pleading.

"Fuck off."

"But—"

"—Fuck off I said!"

Zac stopped. "Ok. If that's what you want."

Leila kept on walking.

Zac watched her march resolutely up the hill and around the corner. He watched her until she completely disappeared. Never once did she look back.

Zac stood there for a while, not sure what to do. One part of him said "Fuck it," go back to the party. Another said, "Feel sorry for yourself. You blew it."

He slowly wandered back to the house, mechanically, while his mind was still being carried along by Leila. He felt himself being pulled apart.

There was a narrow alley that ran alongside the house all the way down to Lady Martin Beach. He took it. It was dark and unlit. At the end he saw reflections of light off the water. His mind began to dissolve.

"There you are," Finn said, as he came out of the alley and saw Zac sitting on the narrow jetty that was owned by the boat club next door. A low fence separated the boat club from the small beach. An upturned dinghy lay on the lawn behind the fence; a pair of oars were stacked up against it.

When Zac appeared not to hear Finn call out, Finn leaned over the fence and whacked his hand against the hull of the dinghy to attract his attention.

Zac turned his head.

Finn mounted the jetty and walked up to Zac and sat down next to him, dangling his legs over the water, same as Zac.

"What's up mate?" Finn inquired.

Zac didn't answer. He maintained his brooding silence.

"Nikki said you ran out of the house after Leila," Finn offered. "I looked everywhere for you."

"Word gets around fast," Zac said. His tone was sullen.

"Don't worry about it mate. By tomorrow, no one will think twice about it."

Zac turned on Finn. A spark of anger flashed in his eyes. "Is that how you see the world? We're all goldfish?"

"I'm sorry. I'm sure Leila won't stop thinking about it."

"You bet she will. And neither will I."

"Nah, you're right."

"Just like I won't forget you stole my idea."

Finn stopped swinging his legs.

"I know you like to think that everyone will forget about that too," Zac said, pressing the point.

"Come on Zac. This is not the time or place to get into that."

"That editor of yours, You're right. She's totally in on it, isn't she?" The accusation fell like an axe.

Finn gathered himself together and got up on his feet. "I don't have to listen to this. You made your own bed, and now you're complaining that you have to sleep in it."

Zac got up and faced him. A simmering rage was boiling inside him. He poked his finger into Finn's chest and said, "Don't you dare twist this around on me. You know damn well what you did. You think that because you're charming, because you've got all your fancy connections, you can take what you want and no one will call you out for it?"

Finn swatted Zac's hand away. "I didn't take anything, Zac. You had your chance, and you blew it. You were all high-and-mighty and said you could come up with a throw-away idea—and then when someone actually does something with it, you start complaining. That's your problem Zac. You've got talent, for sure, but you don't do anything with it. You sit around waiting for the world to hand it to you because you think you're special. Newsflash: nobody's handing out free rides anymore."

Zac's voice was low and sharp. "I trusted you."

"Yeah? Well, maybe that was your mistake."

For a moment, the two men stood there staring at each other. The sound of the waves lapping against the jetty the only noise between them.

Then Zac said quietly, almost as if he was speaking to himself, "You're right. I made a mistake. But it wasn't that I trusted you—it was thinking that you were worth trusting in the first place."

Finn, for the first time, felt something break inside, like a rubber band that had been stretched beyond its limit. He clenched his fists, hard, to the point where they started shaking. "Ever since I've known you," he said, his voice almost breaking, "I looked up to you. But now I can see that I was chasing a mirage. An empty picture frame that I was only too willing to stare into. Well, that's all in the past now. I'm finally free of that delusion. And you just proved it."

Zac stared at Finn with an almost satisfied expression—if it could be called that. Like he had anticipated this moment all along. Then slowly, his eyes grew cold and hard. "You got no idea, have you?" He paused to check Finn's reaction. Seeing that Finn was clueless, he said, "I'm going to take this story to the papers. Tell the truth. And all this money—" he pointed to the Deamer house, "is not going to save your arse. Not even your dad will be able to do anything about it. He'll probably even feel vindicated that what he always thought about you was true." And with that pronouncement, he brushed past Finn, knocking him aside.

Finn stood there for a moment, watching Zac walk off. There was a definite purpose to the way he moved. A purpose he hadn't seen before. And it scared him.

Zac stepped off the jetty onto the short stretch of sand that lay between it and the pathway that ran alongside the Deamer house.

Finn called out, "Don't do it!"

Zac replied: "Just watch me."

In that moment, something exploded inside Finn's mind. Like a supernova. It compressed his consciousness into a fiery ball of ash. All reason gone, blown out into the universe, leaving behind a primeval will forged into a single purpose. He ran down the jetty, grabbed one of the oars laying alongside the dinghy and swung it at the back of Zac's head.

There was a distinct cracking sound as it struck.

Zac dropped like a puppet whose strings had been cut.

Finn walked up to his motionless form. It lay askew on the sand. One arm outstretched, like he was reaching out for something. Under the ambient light, a dark patch slowly spread in the sand around the base of his skull.

Finn looked around. There was just the two of them. Where he stood, he was mostly concealed. The back fence of the Deamer house blocked the view from anyone at the party who might have looked down at the water. The boat clubhouse was locked up. Silent.

There was only the quiet lapping of waves on the sand.

If there was any panic, Finn didn't show it. He could only think of one thing: it didn't happen. It wasn't him. He didn't do it.

The body would have to be moved.

He laid the oar back alongside the dinghy, then went back and grabbed Zac's feet and dragged him down to the water.

There was only a few meters of sand to cross. He backed up until Zac's body was entirely immersed.

And then, to his surprise, Zac jerked, and tried to roll over.

Finn couldn't believe it. He responded by dragging Zac further in until he was almost waist deep.

Zac began thrashing.

Finn lunged forward and pressed his hands against Zac's throat and pushed him forcefully under the water. Zac flapped and splashed about, but Finn maintained his pressure. Gradually, Zac stopped struggling, and finally, he went still.

Finn felt all the strength drain out of his body. He sat down in the water, Zac's body floating beside him. He stayed like that for a while. Then slowly, deliberately, he dragged Zac's body out into the depths, swimming alongside the jetty. He swam the body all the way out to the end of the jetty, then pushed it away.

He watched it float towards the boats moored further out, Zac's face looking up, half-submerged, starting at nothing.

Satisfied that it wasn't going to come back, he climbed up the ladder at the end of the jetty and plodded his way back to the beach. The dark patch in the sand was still there. He used his feet to spread it around so it was no longer visible. Then he smoothed out the trail in the sand where he had dragged Zac down to the water.

Feeling a sense of urgency now, he quickly jogged back up the side alley to the side-door that provided access to the Deamer house. He punched in the key code and slipped inside.

There was an outside shower and some clothes on the line. A pair of short and a T-shirt. He undressed, changed into the shorts and T-shirt, then opened the basement level door that led into the laundry. He threw his wet clothes into the washing machine and shut the washing machine door.

The party was still in full swing.

He climbed the short stretch of stairs to his bedroom, went in, locked the door behind him and went into the bathroom and looked at himself in the mirror.

He looked wild and disheveled. He ran the shower, undressed and got in. He quickly washed himself, including his hair. He got out, dried his hair with a blow drier, got on a new set of clothes and went back out into the party.

Body found in Sydney Harbour

Police have retrieved a body in Sydney's eastern suburbs after it was found floating in Sydney Harbour. Emergency services were called to Bayview Hill Road in Rose Bay about 1.20pm on Sunday. A police spokesman said the call followed "reports of a deceased person in the water." The body was found near the end of a cul-de-sac, next to a public park and a busy walking path that overlooks the harbour. It is understood a resident found the body floating face down in the water near the shore and raised the alarm. "Officers from Rose Bay Local Area Command attended and established a crime scene," the spokesman said. "No further information is available at this time." Around half a dozen police, including detectives and forensic officers, congregated on the sand near where the body was found. The body has not been formally identified.

– 23 –
NSW State Coroner's Court
and Morgue

THE sterile chill of the autopsy room hung heavy in the air, a fluorescent hum buzzing faintly overhead. On the steel gurney lay the body of a young man, aged approximately 23 to 25, his pallid skin stretched taut from immersion. Water clung in droplets to his short, black curls and full beard, remnants of Sydney Harbour still clinging to him even in death. His jeans and black dress shirt, now sodden and heavy, had been carefully removed and bagged for analysis.

Dr. George Whitaker, the state coroner, stood at the ready, his gloved hands poised to begin. His assistant, Emma Reed, meticulously documented each step on her clipboard, her face unreadable beneath her surgical mask.

The initial external examination began with a sweep of the

man's body. His physique was lean but healthy, with no tattoos, scars, or other distinguishing marks. His skin bore the telltale signs of extended water exposure: wrinkled, blanched, and soft.

Dr. Whitaker's eyes lingered on the left side of the head. "Here," he murmured, gesturing with a gloved finger. The man's left ear had been sliced—cleanly but ragged enough to suggest it was incidental, perhaps during a struggle. Below the left ear, a more sinister injury revealed itself: a depressed fracture of the squamous part of the temporal bone. The irregular edges and slight discoloration indicated blunt force trauma, likely inflicted before death.

"Probable cause of death?" Emma prompted.

"Primary trauma to the head, with subsequent drowning," Whitaker replied, his voice neutral but decisive. "We'll confirm shortly."

Moving to the oral cavity, Whitaker pried open the jaw, inspecting the teeth with a small flashlight. "Not entirely unremarkable," he murmured. "Some dental work present." He leaned in closer. "Restorations noted on the mandibular left second molar (tooth 37) and maxillary right first molar (tooth 16). Both are amalgam fillings—older work, likely done a few years ago."

"Anything else?" Emma asked, already updating the report.

"Nothing obvious. Take impressions for comparison and further examination." Whitaker held the jaw steady as Emma stepped forward, deftly handling the dental mold kit. "If we can't

ID him through fingerprints, this could help."

The next step was the Y-incision. With practiced precision, Whitaker made the incision, beginning at the shoulders and extending down the chest to the abdomen. The exposed muscle and tissue revealed the man's inner story—or lack thereof.

Before proceeding further, Whitaker paused to examine the neck structures. "Let's take a closer look here," he said, using a scalpel to carefully expose the larynx and surrounding tissues. He inspected the hyoid bone with meticulous care.

"Hyoid bone intact," he noted aloud. "No fractures or dislocations. That rules out manual strangulation."

"Struck and drowned, then," Emma murmured, as she updated her notes.

Whitaker nodded and moved on. The lungs, removed and weighed, were waterlogged, confirming drowning as the secondary cause of death. When he cut into the lungs, frothy, pink fluid spilled out—a hallmark of asphyxiation by drowning.

"Note: No soot or foreign particulate matter in the lungs," Whitaker remarked, eliminating the possibility of inhalation of anything other than water.

The heart and other major organs appeared unremarkable. Blood samples were taken to screen for toxins or substances, while the stomach contents were bagged for analysis. "Minimal gastric contents," Whitaker observed, "likely the man hadn't eaten recently before his death."

The cranial cavity came last. With the skull exposed, Whitaker carefully removed the top portion. "Depressed fracture extends to the interior," he said, pointing to the left temporal region. "The angle suggests a strike from above and slightly behind. Possible weapon—blunt, heavy, perhaps a pipe or bat."

The examination ended with the body fully documented and samples collected for further testing. As Whitaker peeled off his gloves, he glanced at Emma. "Time to notify homicide," he said grimly. "This wasn't an accident."

Emma nodded, signing off on her report, and stepped out to make the call. Whitaker lingered for a moment, staring at the young man's lifeless face. Whoever he was, his story was far from over.

– 24 –
Ali Baba's
Glebe

"**H**EY sis!"

It was Dano. He was pacing up and down in the back lane behind Ali Baba's, calling out to his sister through the flywire door. Agitated. Annoyed.

Leila came to the door. "What do you want?"

"Have you seen Zac?"

"No." Leila went back into the kitchen.

"Don't bullshit me, I know you saw him."

Leila came back to the door. "Piss off!"

Dano opened the door and lunged inside. "I fucken know you saw him. Just tell me where he is."

"I don't know where he is."

"He was supposed to meet me this morning. He didn't show.

And he always shows."

"Well that's your problem isn't it? Not mine."

"It is your problem—if I think what's going on, is going on."

Leila unconsciously fiddled with the hem of her apron. "What are you talking about?"

"What I'm talking about? I'm talking about your lover boy going to that moron's party the other night."

Leila felt her knees weaken. "What exactly are you saying?"

"I'm saying ... didn't you hear the news?"

"No."

"They found a body floating in the water, just north of there."

"What? No ..."

"Yeah."

"No!"

"Where the fuck have you been? Jesus!"

"I don't know anything about what you're talking about."

"Bullshit you do. You went to that party. He told me."

"He told you?"

"Yeah. What the fuck?"

Dano stared at his sister, saw her eyes grow watery. "Just tell me what happened."

"I don't know what happened. I don't know what you're talking about."

"Cut the bullshit. This is serious!"

"You tell me what happened."

"You want me to tell you?"

"Yeah."

Dano couldn't believe it. He huffed several times to show his patience was running out. "I'll tell you what happened. He came to me asking for a baggy so he could impress everyone at the party. He said he was taking you with him. Did he?"

"I went."

"So you *did* go?"

"I just said that."

"All right. Where'd you go after the party?"

"I went home."

"Alone?"

"Of course."

Dano nearly laughed out loud. He stifled his incredulity and said, "So when was the last time you saw him?"

Leila hesitated.

"Come on, I'm not the cops."

Slowly, she said, "I left early. I didn't see him after that."

Dano slapped his upper thigh. "I fucken knew it!"

"What? What is it?"

"You absolutely swear it was the last time you saw him?"

"Yeah. I swear it."

"Jesus."

"What!?"

"I went looking for him at his dad's yesterday, and his dad was frothing at the mouth. Zac was supposed to spend Sunday afternoon with him."

"So he never came home?"

"What the fuck? Didn't I just say that?"

Leila fell silent.

Dano thought for while, then said, "Whatever you do, don't talk to the cops. Alright?"

"Why?"

"What are you? Fucken stupid? You want to get my arse in trouble?"

"No."

"Then shut your fucken mouth and don't talk to anyone. Alright?"

"Alright!"

– 25 –
Point Piper

L EILA tentatively knocked on the Deamer front door.

About a minute later, it opened. Nikki stood there unmoving. She didn't hide her surprise. She looked at Leila with a mixture of curiosity and discomfort, leaning against the door frame with obvious deliberation, weighing up whether or not to invite her in. The robin's-egg blue cocktail dress Leila remembered her wearing at the party had been replaced by a casual silk blouse and jeans. Despite her apparent discomfort she still managed to radiate an aura of poise.

"Leila," she said with a faint smile, her tone caught somewhere between cordial and wary. "Wasn't expecting you."

"Hi, Nikki. Is Finn home?" Leila's voice was brittle but she maintained a polite facade.

Nikki hesitated. She brushed a strand of hair away from her face. "No, he's out. Meeting with his editor—I think." She crossed her arms and glanced over her shoulder, as though seeking an excuse to close the door. "Did you want to leave him a message?"

Leila shifted uncomfortably on the doorstep. She clutched the strap of her crossbody bag, the same one she'd clung to at the party, and glanced past Nikki into the grand hallway. Everything about the Deamer house, with its high ceilings and imported marble tiles, its exclusive wealth and privilege was worlds away from her parent's modest home in Waterloo. "I was hoping to ask him about Zac," Leila said, trying to keep her voice steady. "No one's seen him since Saturday. I thought maybe Finn might know something."

Nikki's expression faltered, but only for a second. She quickly recovered, offering a practiced, sympathetic smile. "Zac? Oh, I didn't realize ..." Her eyes briefly flickered, betraying an inner calculation. "Do you think it has something to do with—" she broke off, carefully choosing her words, "—you know, with what happened?"

Leila felt the words sting. She knew exactly what Nikki was talking about, but couldn't decide whether it was her fault for over-reacting, or whether Nikki was partly to blame. "Regardless what happened, I went home by myself," she said in clipped tones, "I don't know what happened to Zac after that."

Nikki pretened to take that in, but her polished veneer slipped ever so slightly. "I remember Finn saying something about looking for Zac, but he said he couldn't find him—I do remember that."

"That's why I want to speak to him. Do you know when he gets back?"

"Yeah, right. I'm not exactly sure to be honest. He didn't say."

"I suppose ... is it worth waiting?"

"No." Nikki shook her head quite positively. "You'd be better off calling him later tonight, or tomorrow."

"I don't have his number."

"Right. Can you give me yours and I'll pass it on to him." Nikki ducked inside to get a pen and paper. When she came back, Leila quoted her number and the two of them politely said goodbye.

Leila went back to her father's car, which he had graciously loaned her. A small van which had polystyrene boxes stacked in the back for transporting fresh produce.

As she drove back to Cleveland Street, she replayed the conversation she had with Nikki—or more to the point—the body language that she observed. Nikki was definitely cagey. Leila had the distinct impression she was hiding something. Or at least protecting herself from getting involved.

Admittedly, she couldn't blame her for that, but it only exacerbated the deep-seated feeling she had that something was wrong. She didn't know where Zac lived, but she knew where his father worked. She was still on Woseley Road. She could make a decision to head down to Bondi. She drove on and wrestled with herself. What would it achieve? Did Zac's father even know if she existed? He probably didn't know anything. Going in there cold, giving off worried vibes wasn't going to put him at ease. If anything, he might even get angry and tell her to go away. No, she decided. It was a bad idea. It would only make things worse.

She turned despondently back towards home.

– 26 –
Randwick

Josep pulled himself up from the sofa, walked down the short entrance hallway, and opened the door.

He was greeted by two stony-faced policemen, and before they even opened their mouths, his heart collapsed.

"Mr. Levin?" the taller and leaner of the two officers asked.

Josep gave them the barest acknowledgment. "What's this about?"

"I'm Detective Phelps," the officer said, gesturing to his partner. "This is Detective Mooney. May we come in?"

Josep didn't move at first, his eyes darted between the two men, searching for an alternate reality that wasn't there. Not wanting to move, he stepped aside, letting them enter the cramped apartment.

The officers took in the cluttered chaos—the stacks of books, the heavy aroma of cooked meat, the worn out and sagging furniture. Phelps motioned toward the tattered sofa.

"Perhaps you should sit, Mr. Levin."

Josep ignored the suggestion. He remained standing, swaying slightly like a man on the edge of a precipice. "Just say it."

Phelps hesitated, exchanging a brief glance with Mooney, before speaking. "Earlier today, a body was recovered from Rose Bay. We've since identified it as your son, Zac."

The words that no parent ever wanted to hear. The world instantly bifurcated into the past and present. Cleaved by fate. Josep felt his knees buckle. It was an involuntary response, the shock hitting his body before his brain. He reached out, planted a hand against the wall to steady himself. "No," he said, shaking his head. "It can't be. No ... you must have the wrong person."

Phelps stepped forward, his tone softening. "I'm very sorry for your loss, Mr. Levin. Unfortunately, dental records confirm the identification."

Josep's eyes darted to the coffee table, landing on an empty vodka bottle. His vision blurred as the reality of the words sank in. "What... what happened?" he asked, his voice croaking with disbelief.

"At this stage, we're still investigating," Mooney offered. His tone was more formal than his partner's. "There were signs of trauma, but we can't say any more just yet."

"Trauma?" Josep's voice rose sharply. "You mean someone

hurt him?"

"We're exploring every possibility at this stage," Mooney said carefully.

Josep paced toward the window, and rested himself on the sill. He stared out into the street, but his vision remained blurred. The world receded, all color and sound sucked out of it. His son—his boy—was gone. "How—" he murmured. "How could this have happened? Zac was… he was…"

Phelps stepped closer. "We'll need you to identify the body, Mr. Levin. It's procedure. You can come with us now, or we can arrange for you to do it later."

Josep stayed frozen where he was, as if by doing so he could stave off the inevitable.

"Mr. Levin?"

Josep slowly turned, his face pale. He looked at the two detectives. They were waiting patiently. He had no choice but to make a decision. "Now," he said hoarsely. "Let's do it now."

"We'll drive you," Phelps said firmly. "It's best under the circumstances."

Josep didn't argue. He grabbed his coat mechanically and followed them out. He fumbled with his keys before he managed to lock the door.

On the way, while Mooney drove, Phelps turned to Josep in the backseat and said, "We understand how difficult this must be for you … but if there is anything you can tell us about Zac—his movements in the days leading up to disappearance—we would greatly appreciate it."

Josep, who had been staring out the window in a semi-daze, slowly gathered himself together and said: "He told me he was going out to some sort of writer's party. He didn't say where. That was the last I heard from him."

"What did he do before that?"

"Before? He ah ... he just came back from Darwin. He was away for nearly nine months."

"What was he doing up in Darwin?"

"He said he worked on the fishing trawlers up there."

"What about before Darwin? What was he doing then?"

"He worked as a dish-hand in a Lebanese restaurant in Cleveland Street I believe. Other than that, I think he spent the rest of his time pursing a writing career. He was very motivated."

"Do you know which Lebanese restaurant in Cleveland Street?"

Josep took some time to think about it. "I'm sorry, I can't recall. He brought leftovers home occasionally. But he didn't mention a name. I didn't press him on it. I wasn't exactly the most attentive father."

"That's okay, you've been very helpful."

A medical technician led them down a brightly lit corridor to a viewing room. A large window separated them from the other side. The curtains were drawn.

Josep's stomach twisted as the technician explained the procedure. He wasn't allowed to touch the body, only observe it through a glass pane.

"Take your time," Phelps said softly, standing to the side.

The technician went through a side door and entered the chamber. He parted the curtains. The body was completely covered in a white sheet. He looked at Phelps who gave him the nod. He pulled the sheet back, revealing Zac's face.

Josep's breath caught in his throat. It was Zac all right. Except his skin was pale and waxen, his features absent of any movement. The lively spark that had once defined him was gone, replaced by a terrible, final stillness.

A choking sound escaped Josep's lips, somewhere between a sob and a gasp. He pressed his hand against the glass as if trying to bridge the unbridgeable distance. "That's ... that's my son," he said.

Phelps leaned forward and put a hand on Josep's shoulder. "We'll give you a moment."

The two detectives left the room.

Josep couldn't move, couldn't look away, his thoughts became a chaotic storm of grief, guilt, and rage. Flashes of Zac as a boy flittered passed, as if wound by an old cranked film projector. His mother holding him as a babe, her face glowing with pride. Zac's tentative first steps across the living room carpet, his cheeks rosy with joy. Zac as a boy, sitting cross-legged on the floor, carefully piecing together a jigsaw puzzle, his tongue poking out in concentration. Zac falling off his bike, his small hands clutching at a bloody knee while he bravely held back tears. Later, the passionate bright eyes, full of dreams of becoming a great writer ... and then the stubbornness and arguments. The visions dissolved and the lifeless body hung there before him. As cold and impassive as a carved marble statue.

Josep raised his hands to his face and shut the vision out. He turned and left the room, an ice-cold shroud following in his wake.

Phelps and Mooney were waiting at the end of the corridor. He approached them and Mooney said, "We have some paperwork for you to fill out. Would you follow us please."

They ushered him into another room, an office, and presented him to a secretary behind a glass petition. She pushed some papers at him and indicated where he ought to sign.

Afterwards, Phelps and Mooney drove him back home. Very little was said apart from the detectives promising to do everything they could to find out what happened and would not stop until they had an answer.

Josep thanked them and got out, and plodded his way up the stairs to his apartment. He took off his coat and hung it on the rack by the door, as he always did. A semblance of normality. But nothing was normal. He walked over to the sofa ... but couldn't decide whether he wanted to sit or stand. His eyes fell on the empty vodka bottle on the coffee table. Without thinking, he reached for it, and in a fit of rage, hurled it against the wall. The crash echoed through the apartment, shattering the last remnants of a world that once was.

– 27 –

Point Piper

NIKKI turned her head away and spat a mouthful of cum into a tissue. She had given up trying to achieve her own climax. Promised herself this was the last time she would get dirty to finish the job. Wiggle her finger in his rectum while sucking his cock to make him cum. She wiped her lips and looked at him. Saw that he was a million miles away.

"What's going on?" she asked, weighing up her options.

"What do you mean?"

"Come on, you know what I mean. You're not here. You're somewhere else."

"It's the new book," Finn said, taking longer than necessary to think about it.

"I thought you said you had the plot all figured out."

"I do, but if I'm going to do it justice, I need to actually go over there."

"Is that what this is about? You think I'll stop you from going? Following your dreams?"

He looked at her. Saw anything but insincerity. "No—I don't know. Would you?"

"Of course not. Why would I do that? There's plenty of modelling opportunities for white girls over there. We could figure something out."

"I guess you're right."

Nikki got up on one elbow and really studied him. She didn't like what she saw. "Why do I feel like something else is going on?"

"What's that supposed to mean?"

Nikki stalled before speaking. "You know that girl that Zac brought along to the party? Leila. She came around earlier today."

"Leila? You mean she came here?"

"Yes."

"Why didn't you tell me. Is that what's bothering you?"

"She was asking a whole lot of questions. Where is Zac? Did I see him leave the party? Do I know what happened to him? That sort of thing. You know they found a body today. They reported it on the six o'clock news."

"Really? Where?"

"Floating in the harbour just near here."

"Oh. That's ... that's not good."

"You don't sound surprised."

Finn rolled over to face her. "Why do you say that? How am I supposed to sound?"

"Shocked, I guess."

"Why should I be shocked? It could be anyone."

"What if it's Zac?"

"Woah, hang on. Let's not jump to conclusions. You think it's Zac?"

Nikki held her gaze. "I hope it's not him."

"So do I!" Finn said, suddenly raising his voice.

Nikki blinked a few times, then levelled her eyes at him. "But what if it is him? What will you do?"

Finn took a long pause. "I don't know. What can I do? You make it sound like I'm supposed to do something."

"What if you went to the police first?"

"No!" Finn said firmly. "We don't know if it's him. Going to the police prematurely will just make them suspicious."

"But they will come, eventually, if it is him."

Finn shook his head. "I think you're getting ahead of yourself. We don't know if it's Zac. Until we do, we do nothing."

"Leila said Zac's father was asking about him. He didn't come home."

A shadow passed across Finn's face.

Seeing his response, Nikki added, "Leila was quite worried."

Finn appeared to take this on board. "I can understand. But I'm sure all of this will sort itself out. We shouldn't get all upset about something we know nothing about."

"I don't know how you can be so calm about it," Nikki said, unconvinced. "Have you ever felt something before you knew it happened?"

Finn stared at her.

"Like, I'll be honest with you. When I noticed you changed your clothes at the party and I made a comment about it, you got really defensive. Like I had no right to ask. Why did you change your clothes?"

"Not that again," Finn said. "I told you, I knocked a beer onto myself."

"But why did you need to change your shirt then?"

"Because I felt like it! The old shirt didn't match."

"Since when were you such a fashionista?"

"Oh, come on!" Finn complained. "So now you're going to hold my bad dress sense against me?"

"No, actually, you've got a good dress sense."

"Well there you go. It's another one we can chalk up to the good guys."

"Are we the good guys here?"

"Absolutely."

Finn was grinning. Nikki looked at his mouth, his eyes, and found herself wondering why she had become so serious.

Finn picked up on her change of heart. "Listen," he said, "I'm sure Zac will turn up again. I mean, he's not exactly the most forthright guy when it comes to telling people where he's at. He disappeared up north without saying a word, remember? Who's to say he hasn't done another runner?"

"I suppose you're right," Nikki found herself saying.

"I'm sure it'll all come to nothing."

"Yeah, probably."

He gave her a light peck on the lips.

She tried to soften them, but it felt forced.

He gave her another peck, this time harder.

It made her giggle.

"There you go," he said.

She found herself grinning at him. She wasn't sure if it was because she felt it, or because she realized that maybe she had over-dramatized things a little.

She searched his eyes one more time, and not finding anything there except the old Finn, rolled completely over and looked out at the view.

Finn draped his arm over her and she hugged it to her bosom.

The lights glittered on the harbour. As her eyes adjusted, she saw her reflection in the glass. She felt she had aged. But that wasn't what frightened her. It was her eyes. The sparkle of pleasure was gone. Her pupils were dull and behind them hovered a dark foreboding fear.

Sydney Harbour body identified

A body discovered on Tuesday morning in Rose Bay, a suburb of east Sydney, has been identified as 24-year-old Zacharia Levin of Randwick. According to the coroner, Mr. Levin sustained a blow to the head, possibly inflicted by a blunt instrument, before drowning. Authorities have yet to determine whether his death was accidental or the result of foul play.

Police have urged anyone with information about Mr. Levin's movements in the days leading up to his death to contact Crime Stoppers at 1800 333 000. Mr. Levin, who worked as a freelance writer, is survived by his father and mother, Mr. Josep and Mrs. Ludmilla Levin.

– 28 –
Ali Baba's

DANO waited outside the front of Ali Baba's until he saw Leila was alone, setting tables in the dining room. He made himself obvious, holding up the early edition of The Sydney Morning Herald, pointing to it, leaving her no choice but to come out and see what all the fuss was about.

He walked her to his car, which was parked around the corner in Perry Street. Two of his mates, Mick and Tony were sitting in the back seat. Dano opened the door and sat Leila in the front passenger seat then got into the driver's seat himself. He passed her the newspaper.

Leila read the article, at first pretending like it didn't mean anything. But then she began weeping.

"We're going to get this bastard," Dano said.

Leila shot her brother a fearful look. "No!"

"Listen," he said. "Any time now the cops are gonna find out about that party, ok? Which means he's gonna talk to them. And then they're gonna get a list of everyone who went, including you."

"So?"

"So? Don't fucken give me that. You know they can connect him to me."

"That's your problem."

"My problem!" He thumped the steering wheel in anger. "Who are you protecting? Me or him?" He stared at her with white hot eyes.

"I'm not protecting anyone."

"Bullshit you are. You read the paper. How else do you think he was found floating in Rose Bay? Sailing accident?" He scoffed.

"I don't know what happened."

"You're a liar."

Leila wiped the tears streaming down her face. It mattered little. More tears followed.

"Just tell me what you know. I may look stupid. But one thing I know is people don't do things without a reason. Yeah?"

Leila gripped the newspaper so hard she was scrunching it up.

"I just want the truth," Dano said, mellowing his tone.

Leila began in halting steps. "They were friends ... until ..."

"Until what?"

"Until Finn stole Zac's idea."

Dano gave Leila a cock-eyed look. "He stole what?"

Leila sighed heavily. Wiped her tears away. "They're writers, okay? Zac had an idea and Finn stole it."

Dano laughed hilariously. His boys in the back joined him.

"You may think it's funny, but Finn's book is now a best-seller."

Dano stopped laughing. "Which book?"

"You wouldn't know anything about it."

"I don't care."

"Have you heard of *My Secret Disease*?"

"No."

"Well that's what it's called, and it was originally Zac's idea."

Dano fell into meditative thought for a while. "So you're saying ... you're saying that ..."

"I'm saying if there's a reason for what happened, then that's probably it."

Dano did some more thinking and said, "So you're saying this is all over a book?"

"What's so hard to understand about that?"

"Nothing. I guess Zac was more serious about writing than he let on."

"He was damn serious."

"Well, you could have fooled me."

"Is that what you brought me here for, to tell me how trivial our lives are?"

Dano loosened his neck up. "Na. I just wanted to see your reaction to Zac's murder, and now I know."

Leila wiped her years away. "So what do you know?"

"It explains why Zac came back. He found out he was being ripped off."

A long silence ensued.

Leila put her head in her hands. "I shouldn't have encouraged him to go to the party."

"The party, yeah—about the party ..."

Leila looked at her brother. "What about the party?"

"Eventually the cops are going to put two and two together, and when they do, they're gonna come knocking."

Leila continued looking at her brother.

"And when they do, you're going to keep your mouth shut, you got that?"

"Yes sir."

"Don't 'yes sir' me. I mean it. If you say one word—"

"—What are you gonna do?"

"Just keep your fucken mouth shut. I'm warning you."

"What are you going to do?"

"You don't need to know nothin' about what I'm gonna do."

– 29 –
Stockton Sand Dunes

DANO remembered Zac telling him that the p arty was at a house in Point Piper, down the end of Woseley Road. After checking in at Abbey's in York Street, getting a copy of the book, then looking up the name in the White Pages, they found the address and headed straight there.

They parked a little up from the house, and started a stakeout. The place looked secure; they wouldn't be able to break in without causing a fuss. They had to do this quietly.

Nothing happened until about mid-morning. A cab arrived and beeped the horn.

Moments later, the front door opened and Finn and Nikki came out. Finn seeing Nikki off as she took the cab to wherever.

Finn watched the cab drive away then turned and went back

to the house.

It was at that moment, just as the front door was closing that Dano's boys got their foot in.

Mick held the door while Tony went inside. There was a brief scuffle.

Dano appeared, Finn stared at him, the whites of his eyes flashing, demanding to know what was going on. If it was a robbery, they could take whatever they wanted. So long as no one was harmed.

Dano laughed callously. "You think this is a robbery?"

Finn didn't know what to say. His face registered confusion, and something else. A dim awareness that this wasn't a coincidence.

Dano saw a wallet lying on a half-round table nearby. He picked it up, went through it, and found a driver's license. He held it up and compared it to Finn's face. Satisfied, he said, "You and me—we're gonna talk."

"Talk? What on earth would we have to talk about?"

"I guess that all depends on you." He put a serrated pocket knife to Finn's throat.

They bundled Finn in the back seat of Dano's car, Mick and Tony taking up positions on each side. It was a tight squeeze, but that's exactly what Dano wanted.

Dano stashed Finn's wallet in the glovebox, and drove off, electing to stay silent until they got onto New South Head Road.

Several times Finn said, "What's all this about? What's going on? If it's money you want, I can arrange it."

Dano adjusted the rear-view mirror and said, "If it was money I wanted, you'd already be dead by now."

"Why all the threats? Can't we discuss this like civilized people?"

"Are you saying I'm uncivilized?"

"No ..."

"Calling me uncivilized—isn't that a bit like the pot calling the kettle black?"

There was a tense pause. "What do you want? Who are you?"

"Let's just say I'm Zac Levin's friend. Yeah?"

Finn's face darkened with terror.

Dano observed Finn's response with satisfaction.

"What do you want?"

"Good question. What do I want? I'm still trying to figure it out myself. We got plenty of time. One thing I do know, is by the time we finish, we'll both have the answers to the questions we're looking for. So let's not rush into it. What do you say?"

Hearing this didn't assuage Finn's feelings of impending doom one iota. If anything, he began to suspect he was dealing with a cunning and devious mind, the kind that he had come to know only too well from his research into sociopaths.

When Finn didn't answer, Dano said, "Fair enough. I can see you got some thinking to do. Take your time. I'm in no hurry."

They flowed with the traffic across Sydney Harbour Bridge.

Finn looked out at the view, taking in the glorious shimmering beauty of it. For some reason it had never looked so good, so full of life and vibrancy. More than ever, he wanted to blend into it, become part of it, immortalized forever. It was a startling revelation. All at once, the words his father had spoken to him that day before starting university suddenly came back to him: ... you want to belong, you just don't know it. Slowly, almost as if someone else had taken control of his face, he began to smile. And then he began to laugh. It horrified him. That he should be laughing at a time like this, when his life could be in dire jeopardy. But he couldn't help himself.

"You think this is funny?" Tony said next to him, unimpressed with Finn's behavior.

"No," Finn said, shaking his head vigorously.

"Then what's so funny?"

"Nothing," Finn said. "Nothing. It's just a private joke."

"Perhaps you'd like to share it with us," Dano said from the front.

"No, there's no need," Finn said, slowly getting control of himself again.

"No, I insist," Dano said. "Share your joke with us."

"It's not a joke."

"Whatever, share it."

"Nah. There's no need. You wouldn't understand anyway."

"Say it one more time and I'll stop the car right now and cut your fucken nose off. How would you like that?"

Finn looked at Tony on his right, then to Mike on his left. They smiled at him, their eyes dancing with childish delight.

Finn said, "It's a personal joke. Something my father said to me, okay?"

"I want to hear it," Dano said.

Finn momentarily held Dano's eyes in the rear-view mirror, then averted his gaze. "Before I went to uni, my father said to me—told me—that there are two major forces that govern everyone's life. The force to be free, and the force to belong." He paused for a moment to let that sink in. "And then he said: Everyone has to find out which one affects them the most, and if they don't do it before they venture out into the world, then their whole lives will be a waste."

"So what did you say?" Dano asked.

"I told him I want to be free."

Hearing this, Dano began to laugh. It was a genuine laugh, the kind that is shared by two men in a moment of camaraderie.

"I suppose you understand now why I was laughing," Finn said.

"Yeah, I do," Dano said. "Because my old man told me something very similar when I was a teenager, only he said it differently. He said, 'If you don't get your shit together, you're gonna wind up down the drain.'"

Finn forced a smile.

"So let me guess," Dano said. "Your old man told you you need to belong, is that it?"

Finn studied Dano's gaze in the rear-view mirror. In that instant, he saw a man whose intelligence had been forged not by theories, but by action, honed down by the street into an instrument of discernment, like a blade that was sharp, but not so sharp as to make it useless for cutting through flesh and bone. And, as if by telepathy, he thought he could hear Dano saying: You so needed to belong to the big boy's club that you didn't hesitate to walk over your best friend to get in.

Dano turned his eyes back to the road, knowing that he had hit the mark.

They drove on in silence for a while. The Pacific Highway snaking its way through the northeastern suburbs. When they reached the Hornsby turn-off onto the M1, Finn realized that wherever they were going, it was going to be far away from prying eyes. And that couldn't be good.

"Do you think you could tell me where we are going, and what you have planned," Finn asked, trying to sound as casual as possible.

"You'll see," Dano said simply.

Finn sighed. He closed his eyes, wishing it was all just a bad dream.

They pulled into the Ampol at Wyong. Tony got out and went and ordered McDonald's. Finn asked if he could go to the toilet. Dano denied him. Said he would let him go "further up the road." Finn asked once again where they were going. Dano said that he would "find out" when they got there.

They ate in the car in the parking lot, Finn not having much of an appetite, Tony finishing his quarter pounder with cheese and fries. Finn sipped a coke while they drove back onto the M1.

It was early afternoon. The weather was fine. Mostly blue sky and a peppering of clouds. It wasn't hot, but warm enough to drop the windows a little and let the whistling air circulate.

They hit a quiet stretch near Toronto. Dano slowed and turned into a side road, drove a short distance and stopped the car.

"You can go here," he said.

Finn went out and relieved himself against a tree. Mick and Dano found their own trees. Tony waiting beside the car, having gone at McDonald's.

Around 2 p.m. they crossed the Stockton Bridge and drove through Fullerton Cove. They continued on until they came to the service station at the Lavis Lane round-about. Dano pulled in, got out, and filled up the tank.

If Finn still had any hope, it was dashed when Dano turned down Lavis Lane instead of continuing up Nelson Bay Road. "Fellas, you don't have to do this," he said. He struggled to hold back tears.

"It all depends on what you have to tell us," Dano said.

"I'll tell you anything you wanna know."

"I guess we'll find out," Dano said, not committing himself one way or the other.

Lavis Lane turned into Stockton Bright Track. Dano followed it all the way to the end, to where bitumen gave way to sand.

He killed the engine and sat silently for a while. The rhythmical sound of crashing waves could be heard in the distance.

Finn heard them as well. They were strangely comforting. He had no idea why they had come all this way. What could they possibly want from him here that they couldn't get somewhere else?

Dano opened his door and got out. Mick and Tony joined him, leaving Finn sitting alone in the car. Finn didn't want to get out. He wanted to go home.

Finn heard them opening the boot.

He thought: what if I make a run for it? He looked out the door-side window facing the ocean. Where would he run to? How far would he get? What if they had a gun?

The answer came soon enough. He heard the sound of metal tapping on glass.

Finn turned around to see Mick standing there with a gun in his hand.

Finn's heart sank even further.

Mick waved the gun at him.

Finn reluctantly got out.

He saw Tony standing there with a shovel in his hand. He felt his bowels loosen.

Dano said, "Let's go for a walk."

Mick pushed him from behind, made sure he kept up. They trudged over the sand dunes.

All the way, Finn was saying, "You don't have to do this."

The boys didn't say anything, they marched on in silence.

The sand dunes were mountainous and stretched as far as the eye could see. They could have been in the middle of the Sahara Desert.

After what seemed like an eternity, Dano stopped on top of a sand dune that gave way to the first peek of the ocean. The moisture in the air was readily apparent here. It carried with it the faint odor of sea salt. Close to shore the colour of the water was a pearly emerald. Further out it turned into a phthalo blue. The transition was gorgeous to look at. How could it be, Finn thought, that it might be the last thing he ever saw.

Dano looked at the sand around them. It was partially covered in marram grass, spinifex and pigface. He kicked at the grass, exposing some shallow roots. "This is as good a place as any," he said.

Tony gave the shovel to Finn. "Dig."

"Dig?"

"You heard. Dig."

"I don't understand," Finn said, holding the shovel.

"I'll tell you a what you don't understand," Dano said. "You got involved in something you shouldn't have. And now you're gonna reap the consequences."

"What consequences?"

"Let me tell you a story," Dano said. "When my sister, Leila was about ten years old, there was this boy that she liked. He liked her too apparently, from what I could gather. It was her birthday, and he made this pretty little jewellery box. It was nothing really. Just some cardboard that he lacquered with black paint and he glued some sea shells on top. I think he varnished it or something, because I remember it reflected the light nicely—this was at school. He showed it to me and said that he was going to give it to my sister for her birthday. But she never got it. You wanna know why?"

"I don't know, why?"

"Because there was this bully, you see. He didn't like this kid giving my sister a birthday present. So he took the box off him and stomped on it. He crushed it into little pieces."

"Well, that's ... that's ..."

"So you want to know what I did to this bully?"

"Yes. No ..."

"I beat him to the ground and kicked the fucken shit out of him. He spent a month off school with a broken rib and ruptured spleen. I got expelled, but what the fuck. No one is going to hurt my little sister."

Finn looked at Dano with an appalled expression.

"So, you want to know why you're gonna dig? That's the first reason."

"I never hurt your sister."

Dano looked Finn coldly in the eye, then punched him hard in the stomach.

Finn doubled over and collapsed to his knees.

"You want to know what the second reason is?" Dano said, as

he watched Finn gasp for air.

Finn reached out with his left hand and tried to grab Dano's leg. It was an act of supplication.

Dano stepped back before Finn could touch him.

"Please!" Finn wheezed.

"I'll tell you what the second reason is," Dano said. "It's because you killed Zac. And because you killed Zac, you not only hurt my sister, but you stepped on my business."

"It was an accident ..."

"An accident, yeah?"

"Yeah."

"Bull-fucken shit."

"I swear. I swear. I didn't want to hurt him. I just wanted to stop him from going to the papers."

Dano snarled. "Dig!"

"But I just told you, it was an accident."

Dano had slipped his pocket knife out while Finn was talking. He hitched it under Finn's chin. "I said dig!"

Their eyes momentarily locked, then Finn raised himself up on the shovel and started digging. He worked at it half-heartedly, sobbing with tears.

Dano looked on dispassionately. Mick and Tony lit up and smoked.

After about ten minutes of silent effort, Finn stopped, asked for water.

"Don't have any, so keep digging," Dano said.

"I know you think I deserve this," Finn muttered.

"What did you say?" Dano asked.

"I said, 'You think I deserve this.'"

"Fucken oath you do."

"Did you ask yourself if Zac deserved it?"

Dano couldn't believe what he heard. "You're asking me if I think Zac deserved it?"

"Yeah."

"Is this about you stealing his idea?"

"Yeah. No."

Dano looked at his boys and laughed. "He thinks I give a shit about some stupid idea that someone stole. I don't give a shit about whose idea it is. No one owns ideas. Only God owns them. Who does this moron think he is?"

Finn held his tongue and resumed digging.

Dano said, "You think your life revolves around an idea? Mate, all I care about is the food that goes into my mouth, the pussy on the end of my cock, and how much money you're prepared to sell my gear for. All the rest is for arseholes. You think I give a shit about your life?"

Finn threw a shovel of sand at Dano's feet. "No."

"Then stop lecturing me with your bullshit ideas. You're nothing. You're nobody."

"I am somebody," Finn retorted. "I am Finn Deamer! The successful author of My Secret Disease. My father is a successful banker. My mother a successful gallery owner. I won't be forgotten. Meanwhile, you can have your pussy and your money. It's not going to buy you anything. No one will remember you. You'll be wiped from history."

Dano went very still for a moment, staring at Finn without any emotion. Then he jerked his head back and bellowed out a laugh. "And look at you now!"

"You think it's funny?" Finn said.

"Well I'm up here and you're down there. Yeah?"

Finn was up to his waist. The sand was moist and clammy under his feet. He threw the shovel to the side. "I'm not digging any more. You can dig yourself."

Dano expressed surprise. But it was only for a brief moment. He motioned Mick to come over and take the shovel.

Mick did as he was told.

Dano said to Mick, "Hit him."

Mick raised the shovel and was about to bring it down on Finn's head when Finn cried out, "Stop!" He raised his hand in self-defense. "I'll keep digging."

"You sure about that?" Dano asked.

"Just give me the shovel."

Mick looked at Dano.

Dano indicated to Mick to pass the shovel back to Finn.

Finn took the shovel and continued digging.

"We want it nice and deep," Dano said. "We don't want anyone finding your bones in twenty years' time when the dunes shift."

"How thoughtful of you," Finn said.

Dano smiled. "You're welcome."

"I still don't understand," Finn said after a few more shovelfuls. "I've told you everything you want to hear. I'm sorry about what happened. I can't take back what I've done. It's too late for that. But it's not too late for you to change your mind."

"Why would I change my mind?"

"Because I've still got stories to write!"

Dano found Finn's answer amusing. "I bet you could tell a good story about today."

"I could."

"What would you say?"

"I'd say I was given a reprieve. And then I'd tell the story how I got here."

Dano thought on that for a moment and said, "No you wouldn't. Because then you'd have to confess that you killed Zac."

Finn looked away.

"Am I right?"

Finn slowly returned his gaze. "Sure. I'd tell it differently, change the names and locations."

"But then it wouldn't be the same story, would it?"

"You want to know the real story?"

"Humour me."

Finn rested on the shovel and said, "Zac and I were arguing about the merits of literary versus commercial fiction. I suppose you wouldn't know the difference ..."

"Are you dissing me?"

"No."

"You sure? Because I distinctly get the feeling you think you're superior to us," Dano swept his hand at Mick and Tony. "And I don't like it."

"I didn't mean it that way. I was just trying to point out what I was trying to say."

"Which is?"

"It's not something you guys ordinarily think about, that's all."

"If you know so much, what do we think about?"

"I thought we agreed it was pussy and money."

"So what's the difference between that and telling stories?"

"Nothing I suppose ..."

"Then I'm still waiting."

"What I was trying to say," Finn said, collecting his thoughts, "is what Zac thought."

"What did Zac think?"

"He thought that people who wrote commercial fiction were dickheads."

Dano laughed. "Yeah, he would."

"Well I disagreed with him."

"So?"

"Yeah, but, here's my point. If a story is well-told, regardless how well it's dressed up, so long as the reader gets a kick out of it, if they feel that their time isn't wasted, then I see no reason to put literary fiction on a higher pedestal than commercial fiction. I mean, we're not arguing that caviar on blinis with crème fraîche is equivalent to cheese burgers and fries, are we?"

"A cheese burger and fries can go a long way when you're hungry. But I wouldn't say that to my father."

Mick and Tony laughed.

Finn laughed weakly along with them.

"So what's your point?" Dano said at length.

"My point ... my point is—" Finn said, resuming his digging, "is that writing a story, or a pop song for that matter, it's not something you can predict in advance. There's no sure fire for success. All you can do is suck it and see."

"I still don't get you point," Dano said.

"My point," Finn said, throwing a shovel of sand at Dano's feet—he was getting into it with gusto now, thinking that maybe he could dig his way out of this situation—"is that even though I 'stole' Zac's idea, there was no guarantee that it would be successful. That part of the equation is independent of him."

"You're talking about luck," Dano said.

"Yeah, I guess you could call it luck."

"And you think that absolves you of all guilt?"

Finn stopped digging. "No."

"Then what the fuck are we talking about?"

"I was just trying to explain ..."

"You're not explaining anything. You haven't told me why you killed Zac."

Finn twisted the shovel in his hand. Stalled.

"I'm waiting."

Slowly, Finn said, "What do you want me to say? That I deliberately and premeditatedly killed him? Because if that's what you want to hear, you're not going to get it. I told you, it was an accident."

"Nothing's an accident. There's a reason for everything."

"Everything?"

"Everything."

"Well in that case, beats me. All I know is one minute we were arguing and the next I was standing over his dead body with an oar in my hand."

"An oar?"

"Yeah, a boat oar, you know, for rowing."

"I know what an oar is. What were you doing with an oar in your hand?"

"It belonged to the boat club next door. There was a dinghy there, with a pair of oars standing beside it."

"So you grabbed an oar and hit him with it."

"Pretty much."

"Keep going."

Finn took a moment to reflect. "I suppose I realized what I did, and he wasn't moving, so I dragged him into the water, and let him go."

"So he was dead?"

"—Yeah."

Dano sensed the slight hesitation in Finn's voice. "You killed him. He was dead."

"I killed him."

Dano looked for the truth in Finn's eyes. "And the police? They never asked you any questions?"

"I haven't talked to any police."

"You sure about that?"

"Would it make any difference?"

"No. But I just want to know it you lied to them as well."

"I'm not lying."

"Give me your shovel."

"I'm not lying!"

Dano gave Mick a signal.

Mick stepped up to the edge of the hole and pointed his gun at Finn. "Give him the shovel."

Finn reluctantly passed the shovel to Dano.

The same time, Tony jumped into the hole and grabbed Finn from behind. Finn struggled and began shouting, "Help! Help! They're trying to kill me!"

Mick promptly jumped into the hole and gut punched Finn in the stomach. Finn collapsed limp into Tony's arms, gasping.

Dano threw a roll of duct tape to Mick and Mick wound it around Finn's mouth, tore it off, then wound it around his hands, and finally around his feet.

Finn tried to struggle, but Tony threw him to the ground and placed a boot on his chest. The hole wasn't long enough and Finn was forced into an 'S' shape, half on his side. Mick placed a boot on Finn as well, pinning him down.

Dano began shovelling sand back into the hole.

There was a moment when Dano stared into Finn's eyes, knowing that a million thoughts were racing through the young writer's head. His eyes burned fierce, like a mad man's eyes.

It made no difference. Dano just stared back impassively. It was business. He couldn't care less. He threw another shovel of sand in, some of it landing on Finn's face.

Finn shook it off and sucked in air wildly through his nose. In between he spat a stream of muffled cries.

Dano kept shovelling.

It got to the point where Finn was completely covered, but they could still see the sand moving, like a giant earthworm was passing through. Dano shovelled in more sand, Mick and Tony packing it down as he went.

After a few more minutes of shovelling, the boys climbed out. Dano was hot and sweaty. He passed the shovel to Tony who took a turn filling the hole.

Eventually it was completely covered up. They packed it down by walking and stomping over it.

When they finished, they stood there for a while in silence. There was practically nothing to show for it except a disturbance of sand. The marram grass, spinifex and pigface was uprooted, but that couldn't be helped. It's not like they were gardeners. Nature would do their work for them. There was nothing to worry about.

– 30 –

Ali Baba's

G ARRET felt it was time to talk to Leila again. He waited till after lunch hour because he knew it offered him the best chance of stealing some of her time.

She was busy as usual, but agreed to share a coffee with him, at the same time keeping an eye on a couple of customers.

Garret asked how she was, if she had any thoughts since their last conversation. She shrugged and said "No." It prompted him to tell her what he thought—no beating around the bush, that he had come to the conclusion that Finn had murdered Zac. Clobbered him over the head. As per the autopsy report. Not that it made much difference. With Finn missing, the case had pretty much turned into a layer cake. It was past the point where it was a bad joke. Someone out there had to know something. "I think we have no choice but to conclude that Finn has met with foul play," he said, fishing for a reaction.

Leila fingered the handle of her coffee cup, but didn't say anything.

Garret leaned forward and in a conspiratorial whisper added: "I'll also tell you—and this is in extreme confidence—I heard a rumour that Zac was working as more than just a dish hand here."

Leila's reaction was swift as it was circumspect. "If you're going to make accusations, Mr. Garret, this conversation ends right now."

"I have it on good authority," Garret said. "I'm not going to pursue it—let sleeping dogs. But don't you want the truth?"

"I already know the truth."

Garret sat back, slightly astonished. "Well then—would you care to share it with me?"

Leila studied Garret with a knowing air before saying, "I know how journalism works. 'If it bleeds, it leads.' So let's not play games here. You want an inside scoop, right?"

Garret gave a restrained nod, but it was obvious that he was chaffing at the bit.

Leila said, "I agree with you. I have no doubt that Finn murdered Zac. But if you're asking me if I know what happened to Finn, and my answer is, what ever happened to him, happened for a reason. What that reason is, is beyond me, and I won't speculate on it—with you, or anyone else for that matter."

"God moves in mysterious ways."

"If you believe in God."

"Tell me then," Garret said, reconfiguring, "what are your plans now that all of this is over? I mean, Zac was your teacher of sorts, wasn't he? He encouraged you to pursue your ideas. Do you still want to be a writer?"

"More than ever."

"That's good to hear. Honour his memory and all that sort of thing."

"I intend to honour both their memories."

Garret took a moment to study Leila, to figure out what she meant by that. "That's very noble of you," he said. "Are you saying that maybe there's a story here?"

Leila was quick to respond. "Didn't I just say I wasn't going to speculate? Listen, you're free to write whatever you want—so long as you keep me out of it."

"But you're part of it. How am I supposed to do that?"

"You do it by sticking to the facts Mr. Garret. Don't make stuff up just to feather your nest."

"I'm not that kind of journalist."

Leila laughed for the first time since sitting down. "You could have fooled me."

"No, really, I want to do this justice. It's a mystery begging for an answer. I can't just leave the audience hanging. I want to give them a theory."

"You want to give them a 'theory.'"

"Yeah, something that makes sense."

"You really think this makes sense?"

Garret paused for a moment, to think about that. "I know that real life is stranger than fiction. In fiction, story has to make sense. People won't stand for anything else."

"Because in real life nothing makes sense."

"Yeah, people need to have an answer—anything—even if it is a complete fantasy. As long as they can maintain control."

"And you want to maintain control."

"No!"

"No?"

"No. I would be more than happy with just the facts. But the story, the real story, is why? I want to know why Finn killed Zac. What motivated him."

"You're asking me if I know what motivated him?"

"Yeah."

Leila gave him a canny smile. "I'm not going to be trapped by your mind games Mr Garret. I already told you I'm not going to speculate."

"But this is not about the facts. This is about human behavior. Surely as a writer, you're interested in that?"

"Yes, I am."

"And?"

Leila sighed, but didn't say anything.

Garret said it for her: "I still haven't forgotten what you told me—that Zac was pissed of at Finn for not acknowledging his full contribution. You basically said Finn pretty much ripped Zac off down to the last detail."

"I was telling you what Zac told me. I wasn't there when Zac came up with the original idea. You can take that any way you want."

"Fair enough. But we have to assume that whatever it was, it was sufficient to make Finn mad enough to clobber Zac over the head."

"Sure."

"Because from what I can gather, it appears that Finn was actually somewhat insecure about his achievement. Let's face it, he was an over-preening go-getter, cast in the mold of his father who wanted him to be a successful banker, not some Bohemian artist who wanted to whittle his life away on vapid dreams."

"Is that what you think Zac was doing, whittling his life away on vapid dreams?"

"No, no!" Garret said, shaking his head. "I think Zac was the real deal. Except he was tortured, couldn't decide what to do. But the talent was there."

"While Finn was talent-less."

"I wouldn't say that. Although his editor had some comments ..."

"Comments?"

"Ah, it's nothing—nothing now. It's all in the past. But there was a time when Finn was still green behind the ears. I think his editor hot-housed him, distilled the essence out of him."

"I met his editor"

"Oh, you did?"

"Yes. She seemed to be an iron lady."

Garret laughed. "Maybe that's why Finn's book was a success. She was exactly the kind of handmaiden that it needed."

"I think Zac and her wouldn't have got on."

"No?"

"They would have butted heads, I'm sure."

"You're probably right. Finn was more conducive to being molded like putty in her hands. Zac is more like a hard nut, impossible to crack."

"But once cracked, the nut would have been delicious."

"For sure."

They picked up their coffees in contemplation. Leila swirled hers and gulped it down.

"So I guess it all comes down to jealousy then," Garret said concluding.

"Doesn't it always?"

"It's funny how people who have everything can still be jealous."

"Maybe the trick then, is to not have everything."

"Like not having the whole story."

Leila smiled wistfully.

Garret said, "So what's your plans now?"

"I'm going to apply for a working holiday visa in Japan."

Garret expressed surprise. "Japan?"

"I met a Japanese *manga* artist. He's currently here on a working holiday visa himself. When that expires, he said he's going back to Japan, and if I want, he'll arrange to sponsor me as a collaborative writer."

"Wow! That sounds fantastic."

Leila agreed. "It is."

"Well then I wish you all the best of luck!"

"Thank-you."

On the way out, Garret said, "Thank-you for your time. I'm not going to say this chapter is ended, but I think we can both agree it's a mystery beyond our comprehension."

"Like all good stories," Leila said, closing the door behind him.

– 31 –
Kingsford Smith Airport
Sydney – 2 years later

Nikki Sorbonne sauntered past the WHSmith shop on her way to her gate, and abruptly stopped, her eyes catching a book title that was strangely familiar.

Burning Ambitions.

Drawn like a magnet, she went up to the book, gazed at its cover, and to her amazement, read: Leila Sheshan.

Leila?!

She immediately snatched the book off the shelf and looked inside.

Therein she read:

I'd like to thank the late Zac Levin for inspiring me to pursue my dream of becoming a writer. Without his teaching—which could range from complete rebuttal of my most cherished ideas to gentle encouragement for the vaguest inklings—I would never be the writer that I am today. I miss him greatly but console myself that his spirit hovers over my shoulder, guiding my hand in times of doubt. Secondly, I'd like to thank Evelyn Harper who kindly took me under her wing, going so far as to visit Japan and share my perception of its country and its people, which greatly enhanced the realism of the characters in the story, adding additional dimensions of nuance and complexity to their portrayals. Lastly, I'd like to thank Kenji Ishiguro for generously inviting me into the lives of his family and friends, a gift without which I would not have achieved even a modicum of authenticity. His often insightful observations about the way Japanese artists and writers differ from their western counterparts gave me the necessary perspective to write a story that aspires to be true to both cultures.

Feeling her heart start to race, Nikki's turned to the back cover where she read:

A single spark ignites a chain of vengeance, delusion, and redemption in the world of *manga* artistry.

When Hajime Sano burns down a renowned *manga* house, convinced they stole his ideas, he kills 52 people and is sentenced to death.

Emiko Tanaka, a disillusioned *manga* artist grappling with her own failures, begins corresponding with Hajime to uncover the truth behind his story. Initially sympathetic to his beliefs, she gradually realizes that he based his beliefs on a set of completely false assumptions. This revelation forces her to reevaluate not only her view of Hajime but also her understanding of her own talent and the very essence of creativity.

As their correspondence deepens, Emiko persuades Hajime to accept the reality of his crime and the justice of his impending death. In a final act of redemption, she promises to scatter his ashes into the ocean beneath the Great Buddha, seeking forgiveness for his sins and restoring balance to both the universe and her own heart.

As Nikki read these words, a smile slowly spread across her face. It wasn't just for what Leila wrote, but for what she didn't write. Nikki recalled a phone conversation Finn had with Kenji a couple of days before the party to celebrate the success of his debut novel. It was from that conversation that Finn got the idea to write a synopsis entitled 'Burning Ambitions.' Nikki momentarily closed her eyes and saw the manuscript lying on Finn's desk. In the days following Zac's death and Finn's disappearance, when the police first came to visit the Deamer house, finding her there alone, and interviewing her, she was perplexed to discover that the manuscript was no longer there. At the time, the best explanation she had for its disappearance was that Finn had taken it with him—and that is what she had told the police. But now ... she knew that this was not the case. The truth crystallized with sudden clarity: Leila must have seen it—maybe even taken it.

Bravo!

Nikki took the book to the counter and paid the $AUD23.99 for it, more than happy to pay that price—she would have paid ten times that amount—and walked off into the stream of travellers heading to their various terminals, eventually disappearing into the crowds where she became just another anonymous human being.

Sunday 8 September 2013

Special report by Senior Staff Writer Bob Parkinson:

'Skeleton Discovered in Stockton Sand Dunes'

A grisly discovery has been made in the Stockton Sand Dunes, just north of Borral Quarries, New South Wales, after a local man walking his dog stumbled across what appeared to be a human foot sticking out of the sand, still encased in a shoe.

Police were called to the scene shortly after, where they unearthed the remains of a young male, bound hand and foot with duct tape. The tape extended over the lower facial area, presumably covering the mouth. The body was found fully clothed and showed no apparent signs of trauma or injuries.

Detectives have described the condition of the remains as partially mummified, with the skin shrunk tightly onto the skeleton. Experts suggest the high salt content in the sand likely contributed to the preservation of the body.

The identity of the individual remains unknown, and forensic teams are working to extract DNA and other identifying details. A crime scene has been established, and investigators are treating the death as suspicious."This is an unusual case, given the condition of the body and the location in such a remote area," said a police spokesperson. "We urge anyone with information to come forward."

The discovery has shocked the local community, with residents expressing a mix of horror and curiosity. As the investigation unfolds, police are focusing on missing persons reports from the area and combing through any leads that may provide insight into the young man's final days.

Further updates will follow as the story develops.